Her Knight, Her Protector

Rodeo Knights, Volume 1

Lisa Mondello

Published by Lisa Mondello, 2015.

Copyright

Copyright © 2015 Lisa Mondello

Blurb

Her Knight, Her Protector by Lisa Mondello

As a former Marine Police Officer and rodeo bull rider, Jesse Knight is no stranger to dangerous situations. But when animals in the rodeo circuit start mysteriously falling sick and dying, he knows someone is behind the deed and can't just walk away. Especially when the lovely stock contractor starts receiving death threats. Jesse had been ready to retire from rodeo and settle down on small Wyoming ranch, but how can he sit back while defenseless animals are being targeted and a woman he's come to love is in danger?

Carly Duggan doesn't need a cowboy to help her investigate why her beloved stock has suddenly fallen sick and contacting the local police to investigate only led to more trouble and resulted in her getting death threats. She turns to Jesse Knight, whose training in law enforcement and his knowledge of the rodeo circuit gives him the unique ability to investigate what's happening to her livestock without causing further suspicion. Although Carly downplays the threats to her life, Jesse knows Carly's life is in danger if she gets too close to the truth. He insists on being her shadow to keep her safe. But Jesse can't possibly keep Carly's heart safe...from falling in love with him.

Rodeo Knights includes:

Her Knight, Her Protector, book 1 by Lisa Mondello

The Knight and the Damsel, book 2 by Margaret Daley

One Knight in Vegas, book 3 by Lenora Worth

Chapter One

"What do you mean *another* one of my bulls is failing?" Carly Duggan bolted from the seat behind her desk so fast the chair practically spilled over and crashed to the floor. If her ranch manager, Colin Rodgers, hadn't been standing directly next to her, it would have.

Anger simmered beneath her skin, making her blood run hot as she looked at the young ranch hand standing in the doorway. Thad Ferrer had been working on her family ranch for just over a year and was only a few years younger than Carly. He was too skinny for his tall frame despite the hard work of being a ranch hand. But Carly had no complaints about his performance. He pulled his weight. The anger she was trying her best to contain wasn't his fault.

Don't kill the messenger... She could hear her father saying those very words right now. It had been over a year since Zebb Duggan had stepped his boots in this office, but Carly could swear she still smelled the tobacco from his pipe as if he were standing over her, judging her next move.

Thad twirled his straw cowboy hat in his hand. "The bull this week collapsed in the pasture."

"Which bull?"

"Does it matter?" Colin asked.

She glared at her ranch manager. "Thad, which bull?"

"Cotton-Eye. I think they're eating something. But I don't know what it is. I checked the feed and it's clean. I suppose it could be a virus infecting the herd."

"A virus?" Her heart sank deeper than the floorboards. A virus could race through the ranch and wipe out everything three generations of Duggan's had built on this Wyoming ranch. "What makes you suggest that?"

Thad glanced at Colin and then at Carly. "If it's not the feed and it's not something he ate, what...what else could it be? If we don't do something soon, we're liable to lose all the ranch's stock."

Carly turned her attention to Colin as irritation tumbled forward by leaps. "How long have you known about this, Colin?"

The elder ranch manager sighed but didn't try to hide his guilt. "A day or two."

"And I'm just hearing about this now?"

"I didn't want to cause you alarm unless it was something to be alarmed about. Sometimes a sick bull is just nothing."

"And now we're talking about two. Bulls don't just collapse for no reason, Colin."

He gave her a strong look that made her want to shrink where she stood. But she held her ground.

"And sometimes a bull bounces back from a belly-ache without any fanfare," he said.

"What was the other bull?"

"Dusty Mule. But the bull is fine. It was groaning with a bellyache for a few hours and then grazing like there was never anything wrong. I didn't even have to call Doc Cunningham."

"If you'd been standing next to my father, would you have been so reticent to share this information?"

He lowered his head slightly. But not enough to hide the slight smile that lifted his lips. "Well, no—"

"Then I fail to see why you kept it from me. I decide what is important on this ranch. Don't you forget it."

The smile was gone. She saw the anger simmering inside Colin, but he kept his temper, most likely because he knew she was right. He just didn't want to admit it to Zebb Duggan's baby girl.

"Look, I've spent the last twenty years working with stock. I've seen a sick bull a time or two before. I'll give you that it's strange to have two bulls failing for what seems like unknown reasons."

"They are unknown reasons. We haven't identified the cause."

Colin sighed. "I don't want to be responsible for causing ranches to panic all over the state just because a bull has a bellyache."

She'd grown up with Colin working for the Duggan Stock Company. After her father passed away, it had been a struggle to get all the ranch hands acclimated to taking orders from her. It was clear Colin still saw things that way. Change was never easy. It hadn't been for her. But she wasn't going to sit back and let her ranch hands make foolish decisions that ultimately might destroy Duggan Stock Company.

"The responsibility lies where it's always belonged. With me. And there is no reason for panic since there is no reason for word to leave this ranch until I say so. Are you both understanding me?"

Thad nodded. A moment later, Colin conceded.

"Good. I'm glad to see we have that settled."

Carly thought of Cotton-Eye, her two-year-old futurity bull who'd gotten his name because of the prominent round white spot around just one of its eyes. She saw great potential in that bull. He had a lot of spirit. She hated the idea of losing him.

She turned to Thad. "Call Barry Cunningham. See if he can get out to the ranch this afternoon. Get the rest of the hands to move the cattle away from any stock that appears sick."

"But what about the—"

"I don't care if it takes all day," she interjected. "There is no more important job on this ranch than protecting the healthy stock. If this is a virus, I don't want any more bulls to become infected."

"What is a veterinarian going to do now? It may be too late," Colin said.

"And whose fault is that? A few days ago I might have been able to contain something like this a little better. Now I have to do damage control. For your sake, let's hope this bull really does just have a serious bellyache from something it ate. Either way, I'm not sitting by and watching my stock get sick without a veterinarian checking out all the possibilities. To be safe, move Dogged Ear and Widow Maker to a separate pasture where they won't be among the rest of the herd. I don't want my prize bull getting sick and losing whatever value it has."

She grabbed the phone and flipped through her address book, using her finger to scroll down through the names until she found who she wanted.

"Who are you calling now?" Colin asked.

Carly ignored the fact that Colin was questioning her. She was disappointed in the way he'd handled this situation, but he'd meant no harm. He was an old-fashioned cowboy who still believed a woman could cook on the chuck wagon and be that pretty face to come home to at the end of a hard day's work on the range. It was part of his DNA.

As the dialed the number and then waited for the phone to start ringing, she said, "Melanie Summers."

"The zoologist? What's she going to do?"

"She works for the park services in the Grand Tetons. If there is a virus that is killing animals in Wyoming, she'll either know about it or want to know about it."

"Look, Carly. I can't tell you how to run this ranch."

"I'm glad you remembered that."

"But I have been working here a long time. I've seen a thing or two over the years."

She looked over at Colin and felt a pang of guilt as she put the phone back in the cradle before the call connected. "I know you have. And I also know that my father regarded you as one of the best, both as a ranch manager...and as a friend."

Colin's face softened. "That's why I promised him I'd look after you."

Her eyes widened. "You did?"

He ignored her response. "I'm not sure that calling on people to investigate something that might not need investigating is the best way to go. You know how rumors end up like dry grass fires. Me, hell even Thad, know this herd better than anyone. If there is really something wrong, we should be keeping things in house, if you know what I mean."

She thought about it a few seconds. "You may be right." Sitting down in the leather chair behind the desk that had been her fathers. A chair that some days felt too big in responsibility as well as size.

"For now," she said, glancing up at Colin. "We'll see what Barry Cunningham has to say."

* * *

"It needs more oil."

Jessie Knight sat on the dirt next to a mechanical bull that refused to move. A trickle of sweat ran from his forehead down the side of his face and then dropped to his soaked t-shirt. He'd been working out in the sun for more than an hour and only now had a shady spot in the covered paddock beside the barn to finish the job.

He glanced up at his friend and fellow bull rider, Stoney Buxton, and winced as he tried to force a bolt that was rusted to the metal. *He'd been afraid of that.*

Stoney tipped his cowboy hat back further on his head and crouched down to look at what was giving Jesse so much trouble. "I think it needs more than just a little bit of oil, Jesse."

"I can see why Buford was so quick to let this go. The whole thing needs an overhaul." Jesse tapped the underside of the mechanical bull with the wrench he'd been using.

"Yeah, but when we give it some love, she'll be a good machine for training. It'll do the job right. I just need to work with it some."

Jesse gave the bolt one more try just to please his friend. Stoney was a lot more optimistic than he was about this steel bull's future. He grunted and then to his surprise, the bolt came free.

"Whoohoo!" Stoney hollered, bolting up to his feet.

Jesse laughed. "You do know there are a lot more bolts on this machine, right?"

"First one is always the toughest. Thanks for giving it a go."

The screen door to the kitchen slapped against the doorjamb, bringing Jesse and Stoney's attention to the young woman walking their way.

"Forget about the mechanical bull, boys. I may have some trouble with a live one."

Jesse wiped his hands on a rag and glanced over at Melanie Summers as she walked toward them. She stopped at the rail leading to the paddock and rested her arm across the top, digging her boot into the dirt in front of the area with the mechanical bull they'd been working on was secured in place. It was the first of a few bulls Stoney, Melanie's husband, hoped to set up on the Black Rock Ranch to open his bull riding school.

Melanie's face was serious. "Have you ever heard of a healthy bull all of the sudden collapsing in a pasture it's grazed in its whole life?"

"What are you talking about?"

"I just got off the phone with the owner of Duggan Stock Company."

Jesse stood up and wiped his brow with the back of his hand. "Isn't that the ranch by Cody? My dad used to know the owner years ago. What was his name?"

"Zebb Duggan. He's passed on and now his daughter Carly runs the ranch. She's the one who called."

For as big as rodeo had become over the last century, it was still a small community. If you didn't know someone directly, you usually knew of them. After being on the circuit for years before he'd become a marine, Jesse was familiar with most of the stock companies that supplied animals for the rodeos.

"What did she want to talk to you about?" Stoney asked.

Melanie cocked her head to one side and gave him a sarcastic smile. "I do know a thing or two about animals in the wild."

Being bested by his wife, Stoney bent his head slightly. "I know that, sweetheart. The Park Services wouldn't have hired you on as a zoologist otherwise. But the Duggans run a stock company. The only cattle you ever get up close to are what's here on Black Rock."

"I know my main focus lately has been bison and elk in the Tetons, that's why I initially thought it was strange that Carly Duggan would call me. But she wanted to know if I'd seen any strange behavior lately out in the field with other animals. Something environmental or viral that might be causing otherwise healthy animals to suddenly become sick."

His interest piqued, Jesse asked, "Sick? How?"

"She didn't really want to elaborate on it over the phone so she asked me to stop by so we could talk more about it."

"Strange," Jesse said.

Melanie glanced at him quizzically. "What?"

"You have experience with animals. I'm not doubting that. I'm just wondering why she didn't call a large animal vet."

"She did. One of the futurity bulls she's been showing this year collapsed out in the pasture so she called the veterinarian who treats her stock."

Stoney whistled low. "A futurity bull, huh? She can't be too happy about losing a bull ready to show himself at the rodeo."

"It's not dead. Just mighty sick. The vet can't make heads or tails of it. He took some blood and is doing a toxicology report. I'd like to be there when Carly gets the findings from that report. If it's environmental or something viral, I want to know about it. And the park services will want to know so we can monitor it in case we find other animals who've died. I'm heading out to the ranch tomorrow morning to talk with her."

"I'll go with you," Jesse said.

Melanie cocked her head to one side. "Why?"

"Call it curiosity."

"I thought you were done with rodeo," Stoney said, a slight I-told-you-so smile playing on his face.

Jesse stared at the mechanical bull as if it were a living, breathing thing, instead of a device he'd practiced on more times in his life that he could count. It had been years since he'd been a part of the rodeo circuit thanks to his tours in the marines as a police officer. Now that the marines were behind him, he was faced with what to do next. Being a state cop made the most sense, but he wasn't sure that was what he wanted any more than going back out on the rodeo circuit after ten years of being away.

"Maybe I need a little more time to make that call."

# # #

Chapter Two

"I'm very sorry you had to come all this way," Carly Duggan said. The four of them, Melanie, Stoney, Jesse and Carly, stood in what was most likely her father's office at the Duggan Stock Company ranch. Carly stood behind the mahogany desk with her fingers tapping the blotter.

"I have a few questions," Melanie said.

"Please, have a seat," she said. Jesse, Stoney and Melanie sat in the chairs Carly had moved into place in front of the desk.

"On the phone you mentioned the veterinarian was due with his report this morning," Melanie said.

"Yes, I know. Barry Cunningham has come and gone. He's given me the full report on Cotton-Eye, the bull that had fallen sick these last few days."

"How is the bull now?" Melanie asked.

Carly sighed quietly. "Still not his usual self. But he's getting better and that's a relief. Barry feels he should make a full recovery."

"That's good news for you," Stoney said.

With a slight shrug, Carly replied, "Yes, it is. I think Cotton-Eye has a future ahead of him in rodeo. He's shown well at the futurity events where he's participated. He might just end up being as good as Widow Maker."

"Widow Maker? Really?"

Jesse may have stopped participating in the rodeo circuit when he entered the military. But the sport never really left him and he did keep up on what was happening on the WRC.

"You've heard of him?"

"Hasn't everyone?" Jesse asked. "It may be his first year but he's showing great."

"Nine times out and he hasn't been ridden yet."

"Ah, but your real prize is Tenacious," Stoney said with a laugh. "He's a top contender for Bull of the Year. He's made a real name on the circuit."

"Yes, he has. You've been keeping up on rodeo even though you're not competing anymore."

Stoney glanced at Melanie. "Well, my wife isn't too happy about me breaking my neck, or any other body parts, on a bull. She wants to have babies."

Melanie reached over and playfully smacked him, making him laugh.

Carly envied them. Having someone special in your life was a luxury she longed for especially now since she was alone.

"I've seen you both at some of the events I've been to recently. That's how I knew to call Melanie."

"I'm glad you did," Melanie said, leaning forward in the chair and resting her hand on the desk. "Is that the report?"

Carly picked up a few pieces of paper on her desk. "Would you like to have a look?"

"May I?"

"Certainly."

Melanie eased back in her chair and began to read the report. Jesse glanced around the room as Carly gave a quick recap of the veterinarian visit. All the wood was dark stained and polished fine. The stone fireplace on the far side of the room was probably where most of Zebb Duggan's deals were made. Next to the fireplace was a wooden cart on wheels where bottles of liquor were filled high and set behind fine crystal glasses and a decanter. Jessie couldn't help but think about all the bourbon that had been poured in this room during the negotiation of deals that included everything from the sale of shares of a prized bull to the sperm for breeding if that bull turned out to be a champion like the potential that Carly's prized bull, Tenacious, had.

Everything about the way the office was decorated spoke of being a man's place. Glancing at Carly Duggan, he decided she looked completely out of place. But the space wasn't hers. Not really. There was something petite about her compared to the big leather chair she sat in. Her sandy brown hair was pulled back in a loose braid that fell halfway down her back. The cotton button down shirt she wore was too loose for her frame. But Jesse quickly decided that anything tighter would have shown delicate curves that would end up being a distraction to any of the number of ranch hands he'd seen milling about when they'd arrived.

But that was just looks. As soon as Carly spoke, all thoughts of the contrast in her delicate features and small stature disappeared. She knew her game.

"I told you there wasn't much," Carly said as Melanie finished reading the report. "If I'd known this was all it was going to be, I would have just faxed the results to you. I'm sorry for the inconvenience."

"I'd like a copy of the report anyway, if you don't mind. Just to have on file."

Carly drew in a deep breath. "I realize I was the one to call you, Melanie. And I do appreciate you jumping on the matter quickly. But I hope you can understand that if word got out—"

"It won't." Melanie said quickly. "This report is for my eyes only until there is a need for me to mention it my boss. And then, only if there is some relevance to what we're seeing in the field. You have my word."

Jesse pulled his attention away from the room décor and glanced at Carly. "Something tells me you're not convinced," he said.

She picked up a pencil from the blotter and began tapping it lightly on the paper, leaving a gray lead mark. "It's not uncommon to have a bull die young for any number of reasons."

"But..."

She eyed him speculatively. Her blue eyes flashing suspicion he'd yet to see. "Why is it that you're here?"

A smile tugged at his lips. "Curiosity."

"Just curiosity? You don't have a stake in any of this?"

Carly glanced at Melanie and then back at Jesse.

"Jesse Knight is—"

"Wait," Carly said, putting her hand up to stop Melanie. "You're the Jesse Knight who went on to the finals in Las Vegas...what...ten years ago and then just disappeared?"

He didn't want to be flattered that she knew his name. His rodeo years were many years behind him. But he was. "I went into the military."

She cocked her head just enough for him to see the movement and then said, "Everyone thought you'd have your shot at the World Title."

"Everyone?"

She rolled her eyes quickly and then smiled. "Okay, my father thought you would."

"And you?"

She hesitated for a second. "I was in high school. I wasn't paying attention."

"But you remembered my name."

"Don't flatter yourself."

He sat up straighter in the chair and smiled wider. "Oh, but I am. You and my mother are probably the only two women in the world who remember I was ever a bull rider. And my mother only remembers because she wants to make sure I never go back to it."

"Really? Is that why you joined the military?"

"The marines. No."

She glanced at Melanie and Stoney as if she suddenly realized they were both still in the room.

Her expression softened. "I met your father once at a rodeo a few years ago. He was with Gordon Matthews. Both he and Gordon were on the board of the WRC."

"He's a family friend. Lives near my parents, well, my mother's ranch."

"I'd heard some time ago your father passed away. It wasn't too long before my father was it?"

"It's been five years. Something we have in common."

"Besides an interest in bulls, you mean?" Carly said, raising her eyebrows.

He chuckled and glanced at Stoney and Melanie, who had remained silent during this whole exchange.

"Are you accusing me of something, Carly?" Jesse asked.

"Gordon Matthews may not be the person who chooses contracts for stock companies, but he's very influential on the board. Thanks to my father, Duggan Stock Company has a good reputation of bringing healthy and hardy bulls to the rodeo so there has never been a problem in the past. I'd hate to lose that reputation."

"There's no reason you should," Jesse said, finally getting the meaning of what Carly was saying.

Her gaze bore into him, but he held her stare.

"Isn't your brother Sean Knight, the veterinarian who travels with the WRC?"

He chuckled. "You know he is."

"Of course I do. All stock companies know who cares for their animals on the road in case there is a problem. And there has never been a problem with Duggan Stock Company bulls."

"Until now."

"What are you getting at, Jesse," Melanie asked. "I saw the report. There are a lot of toxic plants in Wyoming that can make livestock sick. Cattle sometimes ingest Larkspur or one of the other dozen toxic plants in the Wyoming mountains. Cotton-Eye probably ingested something."

"Every stock company worth their contracts knows what those toxic plants are. They never let their stock, especially a futurity bull, graze anywhere near pastures that contain those plants. At least not where there are plants in high enough concentration to make an animal sick. A bull is a pretty big animal. Taking a few mouthfuls of a toxic plant isn't enough to cause poisoning."

"True," Melanie said.

"I don't need to see that report to know the levels of toxicity had to be high in order for a two-year-old bull to collapse and need medical attention. Isn't that right, Carly?"

Her lips, a sweet shade of pink, thinned as she spoke. "What are you getting at?"

"Nothing. Just curious."

Carly shook her head. "Out with it. You came here for a reason, Mr. Knight—"

He groaned. "I've been demoted to Mr. Knight?"

"If you keep on the path you're on, you'll be demoted out the door. But I'm the one who is curious enough to want to know what you think you know."

"*Ms.* Duggan, I wasn't just a marine for eight years. I was a military police officer. So you'll forgive me if I'm a little suspicious."

"A little? I think you're a bit more than a little suspicious. You're stopping short of being accusing."

"I didn't mean to offend you. It's in my nature to look at evidence in a different way."

"Is that your way of apologizing for being rude?"

He frowned. "Rude? Carly, I don't think you understand the gravity of this situation."

"And you do?"

"Yes. I wouldn't be here otherwise."

She heaved a sigh that showed her impatience. "Why are you here? Oh, wait. You said curiosity."

"That's right. And I'm also curious as to why you're so quick to pretend your bull wasn't intentionally poisoned."* * *

As handsome and sexy as Jesse Knight was, and Carly was having a hard time convincing herself otherwise, he was annoying as hell. But he was also dead on about what Carly's own suspicions were. And that scared her. If Jesse Knight, a former bull rider who hadn't been on the circuit in nearly ten years could figure out something was amiss, then the board of the WRC could too if they got too close to the truth about what was happening.

She stood up. "I appreciate you all coming by today. This gives me food for thought." Turning to Melanie, she added, "If there are any other developments, I'll give you a call."

Melanie stood, reaching out her hand to shake Carly's. "I appreciate that."

The man was unnerving. Both Melanie and Stoney were standing, ready to leave her office. Jesse Knight sat in the chair across from her desk with his elbow propped up on the arm and his fingers rubbing the stubble on his chin. Stubble that look entirely too sexy on the man.

"Was there something else?" she asked Jesse.

He shook his head. "No, you've been more than patient with me."

Patience had nothing to do with it. She wanted him off her ranch. There was no reason for her to think Jesse Knight would go blabbing to his brother or the head of the WRC board about a sick animal on her ranch. But she didn't need that kind of attention, especially after the letter she'd received this morning.

She heard the sound of boots moving quickly down the hall toward the office and then Doris, the housekeeper that had been working at the Duggan ranch since Carly was a little girl, yelling at whoever was running. "Come back here! You didn't scrape your boots!"

Thad appeared out of breath in the doorway of her office.

"You need to come quick, Carly," he said.

"What is it?"

"Colin and Rod just found Lightning Strikes in the pasture. Same as Cotton-Eye only worse. Lighting Strikes is dead."

Jesse glanced over at her. "Do you still think I'm being too suspicious?"

# # #

Chapter Three

Colin paced back and forth in front of the bull lying in a heap on the ground.

"In all my years," he said, "I've never seen anything like it. No siree."

"This couldn't have happened at a worse time," Carly said, cursing under her breath as she peered down at a beautiful animal that was in its prime.

"Lighting Strikes was having a good year," Colin said. "I couldn't believe it. I went to bring him in from the pasture with all the other bulls we're taking to the rodeo this weekend. He just collapsed right in front of me. Never seen anything like it, I tell you. And I've been at this a long time."

Carly glanced over at Colin. "Have Rod bring the tractor."

Colin was still shaking his head as he walked away.

Melanie crouched down and touched the bull as he lay there. "Do you mind if I take some samples before you bury him? I have my kit in the truck."

"Go right ahead," Carly said as frustration rose up inside her. "If you can give me any kind of an explanation for this, I'll be in your debt."

"I'll help you carry it out here," Stoney said.

They both walked across the pasture to the parking area. When Carly and Jesse were alone, she said, "Colin is right. I've lived my entire life on this ranch. I have lived and breathed stock for rodeos, learned about their nutrition, their breeding, their behavior. I've gotten so I can spot a good bucker before any of the trainers do. My father used to have me come out to the paddock and watch the cowboys buck the yearlings. He taught me everything he knew about how to spot a good bucker. I've never seen anything like this. Lightning Strikes wasn't the best of my bulls. But he was a good bull. Rank. Cowboys loved him because he was consistent and gave them high scores."

She heard the sound of the tractor firing to life and shook her head.

"I can't watch this. Come with me to the office?"

As they started walking, Carly saw Melanie and Stoney walking toward them. Stoney carried Melanie's lab kit. She stopped walking when they reached her. "Meet me back in the office when you're done?"

"Sure thing. I'm sorry, Carly."

Carly sighed. "Me, too. I hate seeing an animal go down like this."

She waved down Rod Nolan, a ranch hand who had been working for her father for nearly ten years. Rod stopped the tractor.

"Just dig the hole for now and then wait a bit. I want Melanie and Barry to check Lightning Strikes before we bury him."

"Doc Cunningham might not get here for hours. Just so long as you know I've got work that ain't getting done while I'm waiting on them."

"Just do it, please?"

Clearly annoyed, Rod sighed and then nodded as he put the tractor in gear. The tractor jerked forward and left Carly and Jesse in a haze of exhaust.

Carly pulled off her cowboy hat and waved it in front of her as if she were clearing a path through the dirty air in order to get to the house. Once inside, Carly glanced back at the pasture where Lightning Strikes lay, feeling an ache in her chest. He wasn't one of her best bulls. But he was a beautiful animal.

"This way," she said, ignoring the fact that Jesse had already been to her office. But anger surged through her as she walked down the hall, making it hard to think clearly.

When they were inside the office, she led Jesse over to the chairs by the fireplace instead of the chairs by her desk.

She sat down on the leather wing chair opposite him. "I've always felt more comfortable sitting here than behind that desk."

"It's a big desk. You looked a little lost behind it."

She shrugged. "My father was a big man. He left some pretty big boots to fill."

"I'm sure you're filling them just fine."

She smiled at his compliment. "When I was little, I used to sneak down here in my pajamas. My mother never saw me. I'd come into my father's office and he'd be sitting here in this chair smoking his pipe and reading a magazine or the newspaper. He hated it when I got out of bed after being tucked in, but he never yelled at me about it. He just picked me up and carried me back to bed and would say, 'Now don't tell your mamma.' I miss him. I miss both of them."

"I'm sure you do," Jesse said. His hazel eyes were filled with sympathy.

"Tell me the real reason you're here."

He frowned. "I told you. I was at Black Rock when you called Melanie. I was curious."

"So you didn't hear this from someone else?"

"No. Should I have?"

"Let's hope not. I'm going to be honest with you, Jesse. I don't believe these bulls got sick naturally. They may have eaten something. But it isn't something native to this ranch or the pastures they graze in."

"Why do you think that?"

"I've never seen a bull act the way Cotton-Eye did out in that pasture. You heard Colin. Even he is shocked. And he didn't even want to tell me about the first bull."

"First bull. Cotton-Eye?"

"No, Dusty Mule. He's a good bull, but not my finest. He'll bring in some good seed money when he's done performing on the circuit next year but it won't be anything stellar. That doesn't lessen my regret for what happened any. No animal should be treated that way."

"I agree."

"But this could be a catastrophe for Duggan Stock Company should word get out about Lightning Strike and Cotton-Eye. Don't get me wrong, I'm grateful Cotton-Eye is getting better. I'd be afraid of losing all my stock if the ranch had been somehow infected with a virus, but Barry Cunningham's report shows otherwise. But..."

"What?"

She blew out a frustrated breath filled with all the emotion she'd held back for the past twenty-four hours. "I don't like not knowing. What if one of the other bulls gets sick? What if it didn't even happen here?"

"What do you mean?"

"Lighting Strike competed regularly along with Widow Maker and Tenacious. Cotton-Eye hasn't left this ranch except for the times we've trained him for trailer travel. When we do that, we automatically pick a place to unload the stock for several hours, let them get their rest and feed. Then we load them back into the trailers and bring them home. Before we can enter them into a rodeo, we need to see if they can tolerate travel. But that's it. He could have eaten something other than the hay and feed we have at one of these stops. The same for Lightning Strikes. Except Lightning Strikes was fine yesterday. He hasn't been to a rodeo in over a week. And I don't yet know the cause of death. I won't know until Barry gives me his findings."

"I see your dilemma."

"Do you?"

"You'd have to call each and every one to see if there have been any other incidences of bulls getting sick. Word gets around quickly."

"And quite frankly, that scares me."

"You didn't call the police?"

"The police would do an investigation."

"As they should. I would."

"Good. I was hoping you would say that."

Jesse frowned, making his hazel eyes darker and blend with his dark brown hair. "Why?"

"If word gets out that I've had two sick bulls with no indication of what they're sick from, and one dead bull, it could jeopardize my contracts with the WRC. I believe that is exactly what someone wants."

"Who?"

She shook her head. For the past day she'd been mulling it over. Breeding bulls for rodeo was an expensive undertaking. Duggan Stock Company ran like a well-oiled machine thanks to her father. But there were always other companies that vied for the contracts the bigger stock companies enjoyed with the WRC.

"As far-fetched as it seems, it could be one of any number of them. It's not really the who that's important."

"Like hell it isn't im—"

"What's important is protecting the integrity of the ranch and protecting my animals," she said above his objection. "I have no idea where my bulls were exposed to these toxins that made them sick. It could have been while on the road, but more likely it was right here on this ranch. I'd like to keep it here."

"I'm not sure I follow you."

"I don't want word getting out about the bulls. I certainly don't want word getting out without having all the facts. Melanie will do some testing to find out if her conclusion is the same as Barry Cunningham's. We'll watch the bulls and beef up security on the ranch." She took a deep breath, astonished at how calmly she could say the words given the seriousness of the situation. "I asked you here because I want your honest opinion out of earshot from others."

He looked confused. But not as confused as she felt.

"My opinion is you need to get law enforcement involved immediately," he said. "I don't understand your hesitation. If what happened out there proves anything, it proves that your bulls weren't poisoned by simply ingesting something they ate. It takes a lot to bring down an animal the size of Lightning

Strikes. Someone intentionally gave that bull something they knew would make it sick."

"I know."

He blinked and then shook his head. "Am I missing something? Are you not understanding what's happening right here on your ranch?"

"I understand perfectly. Someone is out to get me. Or at least sabotage my business. I don't know which."

"All the more reason law enforcement should be involved."

"Maybe so. But what I do know for sure is that what you saw here today can never leave this ranch. If word gets out on the circuit, specifically to Daryl Buchanan, the man from the WRC who chooses bulls for competition, my bulls will be banned from competing and I'll lose my contracts. Rumors have a way of growing legs and making what could be a simple issue into something ominous."

"I'd say the poisoning of your bulls is pretty ominous."

"I agree. And despite what you may think, I am taking it seriously. I'm... sick about Lighting Strikes. I've grown up running around livestock my entire life. I love these animals. But I need to find out who is doing this first without the world knowing about it. It could turn a case of accidental poisoning of a bull into something worse, like a rumor of a viral or bacterial infection on my ranch. I can't have that."

"What are you suggesting?"

"I need your help, Mr. Knight. You were a military police officer, so I'm assuming you have experience investigating crime."

"I do."

"The fact that you were suspicious enough to want to check this out in the first place tells me you were probably good at what you did."

"I was."

She liked his confidence. She liked that he didn't back down from her and that he was still listening. They could work together. "You can help me find out who is attacking this ranch."

He whistled low. "Do you have any idea what an undertaking that is alone? That will require my being here twenty-four/seven."

"I understand."

His eyes widened.

"You'll be compensated for it," she said quickly. "Unless of course you have another job that will prevent you from taking this on."

His expression tightened. "I'm in between careers at the moment."

"Really? Convenient."

His eyebrows lifted quickly as he smiled. "That wasn't the reaction I was expecting."

"Then we're even."

"Was this a contest?"

A smile tugged at her lips. "Hardly. I was merely stating that you've surprised me as much as I apparently surprised you."

"How did I surprise you?"

"You're still here."

He stared at her for a long moment. She held his gaze longer than it felt comfortable. She couldn't help but think of how beautiful his hazel eyes were. How intense they made him appear when he was serious.

"When do you want me to move in?"

#

Chapter Four

It had been just about a week of having Jesse Knight living on her ranch, working and laughing among the rest of the ranch hands in the bunkhouse. So far, he seemed to bond with them, but Carly wasn't sure if they truly trusted his being here. His arrival was so abrupt, that she was sure it looked suspicious.

But no one had asked her about it. Even Colin, who would have been more vocal about bringing on a new ranch hand without his input.

She and Jesse had chosen to keep his real reason for being here quiet. What bothered her more was that Jesse Knight had been on her ranch for a week and they'd yet to discover anything new. That may be a good thing. She didn't want to borrow trouble. She already had enough. But today she didn't want to sit in her office and wonder. She wanted to do something.

Carly woke up earlier than usual and headed to the barn. Thad was already inside mucking out the stalls. He was a hard worker and he'd learned a lot over the past year. It was too bad he hadn't had the opportunity to work with her father. She knew her father would have liked him.

"Are Bitsy and Dobey in the paddock?" she asked.

He stopped his task of scooping piles of manure into the wheelbarrow and wiped his forehead with the back of his hand. "Rod put them out into the pasture a little while ago so I could clean up in here."

"Would you mind getting them into the paddock and saddling them up when you're finished here?"

"Both?"

She nodded. "Jesse and I are going to be taking a ride out to the high pasture after breakfast to check for wild vegetation in the pastures."

"Sure thing, Boss. But Rod and Jesse just did that yesterday."

"They did?"

She must have looked shocked because Thad's shoulders sagged just a bit. "Yeah. There was some barbed wire fencing that needed to be fixed so Jesse said he was going to check things out."

"Oh, well good. I'd like to have a look myself anyway. So I'll let you know when to get the horses ready, okay?"

"Will do, Boss."

She smiled as she walked back to the house. Thad was the only one of the ranch hands who called her boss. Everyone else had been here long enough to either call her Carly or Miss Duggan."

When she reached the house, she was pulled into the kitchen by the scent of bacon and fresh baked muffins. She found Doris working at the stove making a big batch of scrambled eggs.

"That's an awful lot of scrambled eggs you're making this morning?"

"Yes, it is. I have some pancakes too. I even have some wild blueberries I picked myself to put in them."

"Blueberries, huh? You're spoiling me, Doris."

Doris glanced over her shoulder and smiled. "I always do."

Carly chuckled and said, "I'll be in my office when Jesse comes in."

"He already has, sweetie. He's had two cups of coffee and then went back out the door to invite Colin and the boys in for breakfast."

She stopped short. "He did?"

"You weren't up. I told him you probably wouldn't mind since your father used to invite the hands in for breakfast sometimes."

"Oh. Yes, you're right. Thank you, Doris."

She headed to the side door and heard laughter outside. She waited a few seconds and then watched a line of men stream into the house and head to the breakfast table.

She pasted on a smile, feeling out of place in her own home for not being the one to think of this. "Good morning, everyone."

"Jesse invited us in for breakfast. I wasn't going to pass Doris's pancakes up," Colin said, smiling.

"It's a good thing she's cooked enough for an army," she said.

It wasn't unheard of for the men to have breakfast in the house. Carly had grown up sharing meals at the kitchen table with many a ranch hand over the years. They shared meals together on the road when they took the bulls to competition. And when they were working all day out on the ranch, she and Doris would bring lunch up to the hands so they wouldn't have to take time to come back to the house to eat. But it had been a while since they'd all shared breakfast together at the main house.

Carly thought back to the last time she could remember and felt a bit of shame. She couldn't remember. Had she really been so caught up in taking charge of the ranch's business after her father's death that she'd forgotten to invite the hands into her home?

Her father had always made a point to make the men feel his home was their home. They knew he was the authority on the ranch. They respected him. But he was quick to remind them that he had been in their shoes once too. He may have been born a Duggan, but when he was a young man, he had to work the ranch with all the other ranch hands when her grandfather had been in charge of the Duggan Stock Company. He learned everything about raising and caring for bulls that way.

Maybe that's why the hands didn't treat her quite like they treated Zebb Duggan. They knew her father was really one of them, even though he was the boss. He wasn't a man to give an order unless he was willing to do the job, and had done the job, himself.

The men took turns cleaning up using the sink in the bathroom off the mudroom. They all knew Doris wouldn't let them sit at the breakfast table unless they'd cleaned up. Carly headed into the kitchen and walked to the long kitchen table by a long line of windows that looked over the ranch. The benches on both sides of the table filled up with the ranch hands. The only seats left were the ones at either end of the table.

Jesse stood by the table and waited for her to take a seat. She glanced at the head of the table and at the chair where her father always sat. Doris put the platters of scrambled eggs, bacon, sausage, home fries and pancakes on the table.

Carly turned to Doris. "You're going to join us, aren't you?"

"Look at the table. There's no room!" she said with a wink. "I've already nibbled on some breakfast. You all can dig in. I'm going to get those muffins out of the oven before they burn."

"After you," Jesse said, extending his hand.

Carly took the seat at the head of the table and sat down. The rest of the men waited for Jesse to sit down at the other end of the table. When no one reached for the food. They just sat there with than hands in their laps.

"I know you're all hungry," she said. "If you're waiting for me to take the first spoonful, I'm not going to be shy. I'm taking some pancakes before you men eat them all."

She reached for the platter of blueberry pancakes and the rest of the men started dishing food onto their plates. Once everyone had some food on their plate, the table grew quiet except for the occasional request to pass a platter of food or to fight over the last sausage or muffin. When breakfast was complete, Carly thanked them all for sharing a meal with her, just as she remembered her father doing.

"Thad, do you mind getting those horses ready in about a half hour?" she asked as the men started to leave.

"Sure thing, Boss. I'll be in the barn."

"Thanks." She turned to Jesse. "Let's go to my office for a bit, okay?"

A smile split his face. Every time Jesse looked in her direction it was like he saw right through her. It was unnerving. And she was sure it was evident to everyone around them.

She ignored the eyes on her back as she walked down the hall to her office. There had been a lot of looks lately, something she wanted to discuss with Jesse in private. None of the ranch hands knew about the death threats she'd received. She'd decided to keep that information to herself. It may be time for a change of plans.

* * *

Jesse followed Carly into her office and waited until she closed the door before saying anything.

Carly motioned to the two chairs in front of the fireplace. "Please. Have a seat."

They sat down and Jesse couldn't help but notice how incredibly lost Carly looked.

"Doris has been with you for a while?"

Carly glanced at the doorway that Doris had just walked through. "Since my mother passed away when I was eleven."

"You were young to lose your mother."

"You're always too young to lose a mother. It doesn't matter how old you are."

He nodded his agreement. "You two seem very close."

"In many ways, Doris is so much more than a housekeeper. She's been a surrogate mother of sorts for me. My father hired her on as a nanny, housekeeper, and cook. But he didn't know how to do the teenage thing and her duties as nanny outweighed the rest for a while. My father knew bulls, not teenage girls. Doris was always there when I needed someone. She never tried to fill my mother's shoes. Just fill in the gap that needed filling when I needed it."

"Am I here for a status report?" Jesse asked.

"Do you have one? I was hoping you were able to find out if the ranch hands knew anything more. Perhaps remembering someone coming to the ranch around the time Lightning Strikes was poisoned."

"Sorry to disappoint you. These things can take time. Either the men really don't know anything, or someone is very good at keeping a secret."

"Secret? I wasn't implying someone here was intentionally holding back."

"I know. But I also know that in a situation as this, everyone is suspect."

"Even me?"

Jesse shook his head. She was as suspicious as he was. "Unless you have a strong desire for attention, which doesn't seem likely since I've hardly seen your face in the last week, you weren't even on the list."

"I wasn't hiding."

He gave her a crooked grin. "Weren't you?"

Her cheeks flamed.

"Is that why you invited the hands to breakfast this morning?"

He frowned. "Did that bother you?"

"No. It embarrassed me. But not for the reason you might think. It should have been me who extended the invitation. Thank you for reminding me of that."

She took a deep breath and tapped the small area of wood on the arm of the seat she was sitting in with the tips of her fingers.

"Thad told me that you took a ride up to the high pasture with Rod yesterday. Why didn't you tell me?"

He shrugged. "There was nothing to tell. Besides, the reason for going up there was to fix a fence that an animal broke through."

"You didn't see any suspicious overgrowth?"

"No. But then, with Rod there, I didn't want to appear overly interested. I'd like to have a closer look. If we find anything we can bring a tractor up and clear the vegetation along the fence line."

She nodded. "It might be a good idea to do it anyway. It'll take some time, but it might be worth it. Once we're done here, I'd like us both to take a ride up to the pasture where Lightning Strikes grazed before he was brought down to the lower pasture. I've been doing some reading. Sometimes these plants can take hours to show signs of poison in an animal. And small amounts over days could—"

"You're reaching," he said, interrupting her. "The levels of toxin found in Lighting Strikes was too high. In fact, there were multiple toxins that came up in Melanie's report."

"I saw that."

"I've seen no Larkspur or Hemlock up along the fence lines and yet Lightning Strikes had a cocktail of these toxins in his blood. And hardly any in his stomach."

"What are you saying?"

"It wasn't just ingested."

"How could you possibly know that?" she asked.

He braced himself for what he knew was coming next. "Because Sean was here. He not only looked at Melanie's report, but he took samples for himself to double-check."

# # #

Chapter Five

"Your brother was here? On my ranch. After I told you that I wanted this to stay between us?" Carly asked, rising to her feet quickly.

He already knew she hated being one-upped by her ranch hands. But Jesse would risk Carly's wrath before trusting anyone on this ranch who may have had a hand at Lightning Strikes death. Despite not hearing a suspicious word from any of them, he wasn't convinced.

He remained seated. "You know the answer to that. Sean is a vet."

"A WRC veterinarian. He travels with the rodeo! You had no right to call him. This is exactly what I was trying to avoid!" Her lips thinned. "Why would you do that? Barry Cunningham already examined Lightning Strikes. Melanie took samples. If word gets out about—"

"Nothing is going to leave this ranch without you wanting it to."

"It already has."

"Sean is a damned good veterinarian. He's seen just about everything that can happen to a bull. When Melanie's findings were so strange, it only made sense to bring him in. The rest of the bulls on the ranch are healthy."

"He examined them?"

"Yes."

"You had no right to keep something like this from me."

"You would have said no."

"You're damned right I would have." She shook her head. "I know your brother is a good veterinarian, but you'll forgive me if I don't share your confidence."

"I don't really care if you do or if you don't."

Carly reached up as if she were about to grab her cowboy hat, as if she needed a place for the steam building up inside her to vent. But in frustration, she pulled her hand back when she realized the hat was sitting on her desk and not her head. "Now you wait just a minute, Jesse. I was the one who called you to *quietly* investigate—"

"And that is exactly what I'm doing."

"Will you let me finish a damned sentence before you interrupt me?"

"No."

Her eyes widened. If it wasn't for the fact that he was pretty darn angry himself, he'd be noticing how her cheeks turned a pretty shade of pink when she was fired up. He'd be noticing how the little curls of her cinnamon brown hair flattened against her forehead from wearing her hat and stayed that way long after the hat was removed. And how without her cowboy hat, her blue eyes blazed. It wasn't just the anger she was firing at him. It was a fire that burned inside her.

"I beg your pardon?"

"You asked for my help," Jesse said, standing up and taking a step closer. "If you want someone to investigate who is behind the poisoning of your stock, then you need to step aside and let me do my job."

"It was two bulls."

"Three. You're forgetting Dusty Mule."

"We don't know that Dusty Mule was poisoned. Bulls get sick for any number of reasons."

His hands clenched into fists. The woman was so frustrating.

"Listen to you. Three bulls in just a few weeks have fallen sick. We know that Cotton-Eye somehow ingested a toxin foreign to this ranch. Now we know that Lighting Strikes was given a cocktail that could have taken down a herd of elephants. I've been all over this ranch in the last week and talked to all the hands. I have yet to find anything toxic that is naturally growing wild near where these bulls have been grazing."

"My father made sure of that."

"Any ranch worth their name that houses stock would be damned sure they don't have anything toxic near their paddocks too. Someone had to have brought it in, Carly. Someone gave those bulls these toxins. And at least in Lightning Strikes case, it wasn't just ingested, it had to have been injected. It doesn't take a genius to know that it's either someone who is on this ranch or someone who frequently visits. Since I've been on the ranch, there haven't been any more incidences."

He could see her face change from anger to resignation. "Not exactly."

Confused, he asked. "What do you mean?"

Carly reached over to the round end table and pulled open the drawer. Then she reached inside and pulled out two envelopes. "This came yesterday. The first one came the day Lightning Strikes died."

She handed Jesse the envelope, hoping she wouldn't regret confiding in him.

Jesse took the slip of paper out of the first envelope and read the note silently. His eyes widened. He looked at the envelope and turned it over twice before slapping it down on the table. "You've had this for a week and I'm just hearing about it now?"

"I thought..."

"What? This is a death threat, Carly. This isn't just about bulls anymore. This person, whoever he is, threated to kill you."

"I know."

"Who else knows about this?"

"No one. You and me and that's it. I don't know why this is happening, Jesse."

She looked so vulnerable that it broke his heart. How had she gotten to this point in her life where she felt she had no one to turn to with this?

She collapsed in the seat and rested her chin in her fisted hand as she propped her elbow on the arm of the chair and stared into the empty fireplace. "They're innocent animals."

"They're money," Jesse said abruptly. She lifted her gaze to him in shock, but he didn't regret the harshness of his words. "It's the biggest motive on earth for murder, Carly. I'm surprised it's taken this long for someone to take a shot at a ranch like this."

The bluntness of his assertion made her gasp. But given the way she recovered, he could tell Carly knew he was right. But it gave him no pleasure.

"This ranch is run on winnings from bulls," she said quietly. "If I lose the contracts, then I lose over a hundred years of history with it. I'll have failed my father and my family. Not that any of them are left to judge me."

"Tell me about the bulls. Where do they stand?"

She thought for a minute. "Lightning Strikes was new to the circuit this year. He had a promising future, just like Widow Maker. Widow Maker has been out seven times and is unridden. And Tenacious has been having a good year. He's in line for Bull of the Year. You know what that kind of notoriety that can have on the value of a bull. Moneywise, I mean."

"Yes, I do."

"There is a sponsor who is interested. It's the kind of attention all stock companies work for. But all that could be lost if word gets out."

"Is that why you didn't tell me about the death threats?"

She shook her head. "I don't know. I guess I wanted to believe it was just random and would just stop like the poisonings. I was trying to protect the ranch."

"By leaving yourself exposed? No. You should have told me when you got the first letter. The day I agreed to help you. I would have treated this totally different."

"How?"

"For one, I wouldn't have left you alone in this big house where anyone could get to you. The damned doors are kept unlocked all day and all night."

"My father had an open door policy with the hands. He didn't want this to be a fortress they weren't welcome in."

"As of today, the doors are closed and locked at all times when you're in the house."

"What?"

"And despite what you think about my brother and my family involvement with the WRC, I need people around me I know I can trust to have my back. That's the only way I can ensure your safety and the safety of your animals."

"What are you suggesting?"

"When you're scheduled for a rodeo, we'll take the bulls to my family ranch in Montana for any layovers. My mother's ranch is close enough. There's plenty of room to house the bulls in an environment we know is safe."

"And when they're not leaving the ranch for a rodeo?"

"I want my brother Sean to have access to all the bulls and perform random examinations. He's a good large animal veterinarian. We don't' know which bull, if any, will be targeted next. He can take blood samples. Perhaps the mere appearance of him on the ranch will keep someone from making another move."

"Can I count on you for discretion in not letting this get back to the WRC?"

"You have my word."

She stared at him for a moment. "What about your brothers?"

With a slight grin, he said, "Carly, we all come from the same stock."

She stood up and took a step toward him. A wave of spearmint hit his senses. "Jesse, you do understand the future of this ranch depends on it, don't you?"

He didn't want to be annoyed. He'd already given her his word. As a marine, that meant something. But to Carly Duggan, that was clearly not enough.

"You don't know me that well," he said. "But you will. I still think you should go to the police with this, Carly. In fact, I think you've acted foolish where your safety is concerned."

"I don't expect you to understand my position, Jesse. You're a man. And while I know that sounds sexist, I also know you've never been on the receiving end of being told you're a paranoid girl who doesn't belong in this business."

He laughed and felt it deep in his belly. When she flashed him an annoyed expression, he said, "Sorry. I'm not laughing at you. Really, I'm not. I was just thinking that if my mother were standing in the room and I accused you of something like that, she'd be giving me a warning stare more scary than anything you could dish out to me for forgetting that."

"I'd probably like your mother then."

"You would. She's a strong woman. I also know that anyone who would think you were paranoid in this situation is nothing but an idiot."

She chuckled and he loved the way it transformed her whole face.

"You don't laugh enough."

She still held her laugh, but seemed self-conscious. "There hasn't been a whole lot to laugh about lately."

"Maybe we can change that on our ride up to the pasture. No one will be around to judge you except me. And you won't get that from me."

He towered over Carly Duggan as he suspected her father, the man whose portrait was hanging in the office, probably did. But he had no desire to intimidate her or make her feel scared or small. He liked her. He liked that she didn't back down to him and she held herself strong. He still believed she'd been incredibly irresponsible in not telling him about the death threats. But now that he knew about them, he knew what to do.

"You hire me as a ranch hand here on the ranch. That covers my being able to walk freely around your crew and hear whatever conversations they're having. Being in the bunkhouse has produced nothing. Those death threats trump whatever information they may have been holding back if they did know something. You need to trust me to do this my way. No questions."

She sighed. "That's hard for me."

"I know. You don't know me enough to trust me. But I don't need your trust or the trust of your men to do my job and keep you safe."

"How do you suggest we handle this?"

"The way I see it is, we stop hiding it. Your men already know the bulls were poisoned. They should know why I'm really here. No whispers. No pretense."

"You mean tell them about the death threats?"

"Yes. And tell them that I'm in charge."

When she straightened her spine, he held up a hand.

"You're running the ranch, Carly. I'm running this investigation."

She rubbed her temple as if she were trying to ease out a sore spot. Then she looked at him.

"Were you a good cop?"

"MP? Yes."

"Soldier?"

"Soldiers are in the army. I was a marine."

Her lips lifted on one side. "My mistake."

"It's a common one."

She got up and walked behind the mammoth desk that seemed so out of place for her. Jesse knew that Zebb Duggan had died just about a year ago. He glanced around the room and deduced that Carly had probably kept the office exactly the same as it had been when he'd been alive.

"There probably isn't much reason for you to stay in the bunkhouse anymore."

"No. In fact, given the change of status, I would prefer to sleep in the room next to yours. Though I doubt I'll get much sleep with you being right in the next room."

Her cheeks turned a sweet shade of pink and her lips tilted just enough to show him she was flattered. He was right to guess that he was better off sleeping elsewhere. His fingers itched to touch her cinnamon brown hair and push back the little curls that had pasted themselves on her forehead, a result of her wearing her cowboy hat before breakfast.

"Of course, that might change," he added.

"What? That you'll get sleep? I hope so. I want you rested if you're going to be working here on the ranch."

His insides turned with thoughts he didn't want to have. "No, the part about sleeping here in the room next to yours."

She gave him a harsh glance. "I don't invite strangers into my bedroom, if that's what you're thinking."

"The thought of that, while enticing, is not what I'm talking about. And you wound me. I didn't think we were strangers anymore. But if you get any more death threats, I'm going to want to make sure you have protection, both outside on the grounds and in this house. I'll want to bring in security."

Her eyes widened. "Oh. Do you really think it will get that far? I've been assuming whoever sent me those letters were just a way to scare me."

"Carly, this person, whoever it is, killed one of your bulls and has now threatened your life. They didn't ask you to be prom queen. And this may not be the end of it. I don't want to find out the hard way. Do you?"

He glanced down at the words on the page again as if he needed to read them again to believe them. She understood. She'd probably read the letter a hundred times since she'd opened it.

"No." She got up from the chair and paced a few times. "The locked doors...we might get some resistance from the hands. They're used to being able to come into the office at will to talk with me or to even get a snack that Doris leaves out for them."

"I don't care. Change is never easy. Do you think they'll defy you?"

She snapped a sharp look in his direction. "On this ranch, I expect my hands to follow my orders. Otherwise, they're gone."

It wasn't that simple. But given the circumstances, Jesse knew it was better to stay close to Carly in order to make sure no one made good on those threats. Carly trusted Colin to handle the business of the bulls with her workers.

"I think it's time for some honesty with the ranch hands and to get everyone on board with these changes."

# # #

Chapter Six

The talk with the ranch hands had gone about as well as Carly had expected. Thad was nervous about the death threats. Colin was angry she'd never told him about it. She couldn't exactly blame Colin for being angry. She should have trusted him. And when she'd looked at his face as Jesse explained what was going on, all Carly saw was betrayal. She hadn't trusted him. She should have.

As she'd expected, the ride up to the high pasture had not only eased some of her anxiety, it had given her just a little bit of the distance she needed from the ranch to finally forget about the death threats for a moment.

Bitsy, her favorite mare, was leading the way through the pasture so Carly didn't have to think about anything except the sun shining on her hat and the man riding on the horse next to hers.

"You're deep in thought," Jesse said after they'd ridden for a while.

"Yeah."

"You sound sad."

She sighed. "Not sad. Well, maybe a little. I hate hurting Colin's feelings. We may have had a bit of a rough go this year since my father passed away, but I shouldn't have kept him out of the loop on what was happening. He felt betrayed. I could see it in his eyes when you were the one to tell him about the death threats. Since my father's death, he's looked after me some. He didn't deserve the way I treated him."

"Stop being so hard on yourself. Life's not easy sometimes."

She glanced over at Jesse. He sat tall in the saddle. And handsome with his dark hair that she could see underneath his Stetson, and shoulders that were wide enough to make a woman feel tiny and secure.

"That's true enough."

"How long has he been with the ranch?"

"Since I was a little girl. You know, he was the one to teach me to ride a bike?"

"Yeah?"

"I could ride a horse all day long but I couldn't ride a bike. So he taught me."

Jesse chuckled. "A jack of all trades. Does he have any kids of his own?"

"No, Colin never married. I asked Doris about it once. She said he'd been in love with a woman when he was a young man but she ended up marrying someone else. It broke his heart so much that he never went looking for love after that."

"Wow."

"He was a good friend of my father's. He knew his place on the ranch. But when my mother died, Colin was the one who really helped pull him out of his depression. He drank too much and didn't care about the ranch. Colin pushed him. Eventually my dad was able to move on."

"I wish my mother would."

"What do you mean?"

She glanced over at Jesse. He stared out at the pasture ahead of them and then at her. His eyes were glassy, as if he were about to cry.

"She'll never get over losing my dad. She loved him right from the beginning. She'll love him and only him until we bury her. I just hate the idea of her being alone."

"She has her boys. Does she ever go out with friends?"

He shook his head. "Well, Gordon."

"Gordon. Gordon Matthews?"

"They're companions. Mostly because they've lived next to each other for so long. But...no."

"No what?"

"I can't see it."

"You mean you can't see them becoming romantically involved?"

He shook his head again as if it was too strange to think about. "He's been married a few times and divorced. My mom is a one man woman."

"Really? Have you filled her in on that yet?"

He glanced at her quickly. At first, he seemed confused. But then he smiled. "You think I'm being ridiculous."

She shook her head. "Actually, I know what you're saying. For a long time I wished that Doris and my father would fall in love and get married. But that wasn't meant to be. They were comfortable just being friends."

He stared out at the horizon in thought for a second. "Yeah, I guess that's pretty much the way it's been for my mother and Gordon. Comfortable companions.

"She misses my father. I miss him. I never thought I could miss anyone so much. He died while I was still in the military. Getting that call was like a dagger to my heart."

He seemed so naked when he spoke of his father. And yet, he didn't seem at all uncomfortable with revealing this side of himself.

"I do understand what you mean," she said.

He gave her a weak smile. "I know you do."

They reached a shady spot along the fence line.

"There's a brook up ahead. If you want we can stop and let the horse drink for a bit," she said.

When they reached the brook, Jesse quickly dismounted and loosely wrapped the reins around the saddle horn. Then he let Dobey walk to the brook. She was just about to do the same, when Jesse came up alongside of Bitsy and reached his arms up to her.

"I can dismount myself," she said.

"I know you can. But that doesn't mean you can't except help when it's offered."

She didn't want to delve into the deeper meaning of that. Surely he knew that she'd lived her whole life on this ranch. She couldn't count the number of times she'd climbed into a saddle and dismounted.

But Jesse's arms where still extended and something about the gentlemanly way he looked after her made her heart sing. It was completely unnecessary and even a little annoying. But it also made Carly feel special in a way she hadn't felt in a very long time. Only she couldn't recall ever feeling this way at all.

Holding on to the saddle horn, she put her weight on her left foot and swung her right leg over the saddle and let it fall until she felt the ground below. Jesse's hands were there, holding her by the waist to steady her, even though she didn't need it. His hands remained around her waist until she loosely wrapped the reins around Bitsy saddle horn and let her walk to the brook to take a drink.

She turned around and looked up at him. The sun was behind him, making it hard to make out the features of his face.

"Something tells me it wasn't such a good idea for us to ride up here alone," Jesse said.

"Why?"

"Because…I want to kiss you Carly. I've wanted to kiss you since the moment I stepped into your office that first day."

"Really?"

He sighed as if he were frustrated with himself more than anything. "But that probably wouldn't be the smartest thing I've ever done."

"Probably not," she said quietly, feeling a disappointment that was foreign to her.

She stepped away into the shady area and took a deep breath. The shade was a nice change over the heat of the sun and being on the back of a hot horse. Carly pulled off her cowboy hat and walked toward the fence line as if she had a purpose. She didn't. She just didn't want to face Jesse.

"I'm sorry. I shouldn't have said that."

She turned around quickly and saw Jesse still standing in the spot where she'd fled from. "Which part?"

"The part about kissing you. I've offended you."

She felt offended, but only because the kiss never happened.

"Forget it. Let's look at the fence line."

She pretended to inspect the vegetation in the surrounding around. When Jesse walked past her, it was a relief. She'd felt his eyes on her and she just didn't want to feel that exposed.

Jesse looked around. "If there was going to be any overgrowth, it would be by the brook where the water could feed it."

"I don't see anything. Most of the poisonous plants on this mountain would be blooming right now. But I don't see any flowers in the pasture."

The moment was gone. The beautiful expression of emotion when Jesse spoke of his parents' love, and then the heartache of learning about his father's death had given her a glimpse of this man that she longed to see more of. And then he'd unabashedly admitted he wanted to kiss her.

And then he didn't.

She stared at the bare ground and felt more disappointment over what was lost in those brief moments than any happiness over not finding any poisonous plants.

# # #

Chapter Seven

They spent the next few days making trips to Jesse's brother Michael's ranch in Montana. As suspected, none of the hands were happy about the changes in rules on the ranch, or that Jesse had been watching their every move in the bunkhouse.

Carly couldn't really blame them. Jesse had been right. She should have been honest about the death threats right from the beginning. Colin, more than any of them, was most worried when he'd heard about the letters.

She couldn't deny that she was comforted by the fact that Jesse was sleeping in the next room. She hadn't realized just how tired she'd become by trying to handle all that had been going on these last few weeks by herself. But it was more than that. The memory of the way Jesse looked at her and smiled when they were riding still melted her heart. She'd lay awake in bed just thinking of the feel of his hands on her waist as he gently helped her down from her horse. Not that he needed to. Carly had grown up taking spills from many a horse in her lifetime. It went part and parcel with living on a ranch.

But more than his strength and his smile, she couldn't shake the way he'd been vulnerable with her while talking about his father. Most of the men Carly knew, including her own dad, kept their feelings hid. It had always made her think she was weak for showing her emotions, that she'd be judged for them. But Jesse wore them on his sleeve without any shame.

Yes, Jesse Knight was a different kind of man. A gentlemen and a gentle soul filled with honor.

They were getting ready for their next rodeo with fifteen of her bulls in competition. Rodeo day was always an exciting day and today was no different.

The trailer with the bulls that were going to compete in Montana had already left the ranch and stayed the night at Jesse's brother Michael's ranch. Colin had gone with them, but didn't know where they were going until Michael had arrived with Stoney to drive the trailer up to the arena. The rest of the hands stayed behind, leaving a lot of talk. But Doris wasted no time enlisting both Thad and Rod to help her with her monthly grocery shopping. All that was left was for her to get ready and drive the few hours up to Bozeman for the competition.

Carly sat at the vanity table her mother had picked out for her when she was just eight years old. Every girl needs a vanity, she'd said. Carly had been too young then to understand what she meant. Back then she used it as a place to draw pictures with her crayons. It was only long after her mother had died that Carly appreciated the gift her mother had given her. There wasn't a day she sat at the vanity that she didn't think of some special moment with her.

She opened the jar of her favorite hand cream and saw that it was full, which made her think for a minute. She'd mentioned to Doris that she was running low. Doris most likely picked up a few jars when she'd gone shopping with the ranch hands.

Carly inhaled the spearmint scent of the cream and then slathered it on her hands and wrists. Even when she wasn't working around the ranch, her hands were always dry. It only got worse in the wintertime when the heat from the stoves in the main house sucked all the moisture out of her body.

Carly was just screwing on the lid to the jar of cream when she heard a knock on her bedroom door. Expecting it to be Jesse, her heart lifted a notch.

"Come in," she said.

Seconds later, Doris walked in with a stack of towels in her hand. "Oh, I'm sorry, sweetheart. I saw the truck pulled up to the door out front and thought you were on your way already."

"Jesse pulled the truck up to the door?" Carly asked as she stood.

Doris chuckled. "That boy was raised right. Definitely a keeper."

Carly quickly rolled her eyes at Doris's teasing. "He's definitely something all right."

Doris was halfway to the en suite bathroom with the towels when she stopped and turned to Carly. "Don't you dare tell me you don't think he's handsome because I know better."

"I never said that."

"And he's built like a—"

"Doris! There are plenty of strong men on this ranch," Carly argued.

"And he can't keep his eyes off of you. If given the chance, it wouldn't be the only thing he can't keep off you."

"Doris! What has gotten into you?"

The housekeeper's expression changed from amusement to the same warmth and concern Carly remembered when she was a teen and was missing her mother. "I like seeing you smile. It's been too long. I know the job you have here is a mighty one. But it's okay to remember you're also a woman, sweetie. You can experience something other than trying to make your father proud of you. He was proud of you. Always. Having something, or someone, for yourself is never going to change that."

"I'm not so sure about that."

"Your father was a man. All men have a hard time letting their little girls grow up. If he'd had his way, you would have stayed eleven years old forever."

Tears filled her eyes. "You're probably right."

"I know I am. Just like I know that man out there will wait all afternoon for you to come out of this room and still give you a smile as if he hadn't wasted half the day."

Carly chuckled softly as she thought of Jesse. "I think you're exaggerating."

"Yeah? He's been sitting in that hot truck for a half hour already waiting on you."

* * *

Her stomach rolled each time the truck hit a bump on the highway up to Bozeman, Montana. Normally Carly enjoyed the ride. The anticipation of seeing one of her bulls perform well was always a treat. Both Tenacious and Widow Maker were going to compete today and she wanted to be there to see their scores. Tenacious was in the running for Bull of the Year, and when that happened, it would bring more attention to the Duggan Stock Company and make seeding shares rise for both bulls. Widow Maker was showing well and Carly was hopeful the young bull would follow in the footsteps of her prized bull.

But the closer they got to the arena in Bozeman, the sicker Carly felt. She was glad she let Jesse drive. Maybe if she just put her head back against the headrest for a little while, she'd feel better.

"Are you going to be able to last the day?"

Beads of sweat bubbled up on her forehead, making her cold. "I guess I didn't sleep very well last night. I just need a few minutes."

"We still have a few hours before we reach Bozeman. Kick back and take a nap. I'll wake you when we get close."

She felt her heart beating in her chest and drew in a deep breath to steady herself. "I think I'll do just that."

The next thing she knew, Jesse was shaking her awake. "We're here, sleepyhead."

If the sound of his voice inside the cab of the truck wasn't enough to rouse her, the sound of the crowd and the announcer's voice coming over the loudspeaker would have.

"We just made it," she said as she looked around and processed her surroundings in her hazy state.

"How are you feeling?"

She touched her face and felt the warmth of her skin. "Surprisingly good. I guess all I needed was a little sleep."

"Good. Then it should be a good day." Jessie climbed out of the truck and came around to the passenger side before she had a chance to get out. He opened the door. In a low voice, he added, "I want you to stay close to me. There are a lot of people here and we still don't know who to trust."

She stepped out of the truck and Jesse slammed the door.

"I'm worried about my bulls."

"Sean and Bobby are here. Stoney and Melanie are here, too. Stoney is going to stay around the chute area. Michael is in the back with all the bulls."

"Bobby is Sean's intern, right?"

"Yes."

"Does Bobby know what happened at the ranch?"

Jesse shook his head. "Sean didn't tell him. You said you don't want to hide. This is the best way I can think of having you participate like you usually do without putting you at risk."

Nerves raced through her as they walked to the arena. No one here had visited the ranch recently. But that's not to say that the death threat letters she'd received weren't from someone who could be here today. Jesse was right. It was best to be suspicious of everyone until they knew for sure how the poisonings on the ranch occurred.

She said hello to a few of the people on the circuit that she knew well as they moved through the crowd and then found a spot in the stands to watch the show. As Jesse mentioned, Stoney was standing on the arena floor behind the chute with a few other cowboys who were competing today. He blended in because he knew most all of the cowboys who were competing and had competed with them until last year when he'd retired for good.

Jesse leaned into her. She felt the heat of his body and inhaled a hint of his aftershave. The same scent that had been teasing her nose the entire time she'd been in the cab of the truck.

"Relax and just enjoy the show."

"That's easy for you to say."

But it didn't take long for Carly to relax and get into the competition. She was always interested in watching the bulls that the other stock companies brought to the show just as much as she enjoyed rooting for her own bulls. She watched the bulls and the cowboys just as intently as Jesse did. They talked with each other about riding form and the characteristic of the bulls they'd seen. When the next cowboy was called for a ride, she knew Tenacious was up.

"I hold my breath every time Tenacious is in the chute," she said.

The cowboy climbed into the chute and took a few minutes to adjust his flank strap. Carly could see the tension building in Tenacious. She knew him so well that she could anticipate exactly how he'd turn. He was ready to bolt. It meant this cowboy was in for a good ride.

The chute opened and Tenacious bolted out of the chute, kicking, twisting and doing everything he needed to do to get this cowboy off his back. Dust was kicking up from the ground and off the bull's back. The cowboy, a veteran bull rider who was looking for a good score, was hanging in there. After six seconds, the cowboy lost his seat and slipped just enough so the next buck Tenacious delivered sent him flying to the ground. Two bull fighters moved in to distract Tenacious until the cowboy was able to scramble away to the safety of the arena fence.

Carly couldn't hold back the smile that split her face.

"Congratulations."

The deep voice coming from behind them on the bleachers had her turning with dread. Gordon Matthews sat on the end of the bleachers, smiling down at her.

"I thought the board members of the WRC had special seats. What are you doing in the stands with us lowly people?" Jesse joked.

Gordon laughed. "Lowly? These are the best seats in the house. I like watching from up here. You see more."

Carly agreed. It's exactly why she always chose a seat higher up in the stands to watch the show.

"What's the congratulations for?" Jesse asked.

"It's for Carly. She earned another five hundred dollars with that run for Duggan Stock Company."

Gordon referred to the bonus bull owners got every time one of their bulls bucked off a bull rider.

"Tenacious is earning you some money this year," he added.

"He's having a good year," Carly said, feeling the pride of having a bull that people were taking notice of on the circuit. "I hear you've got some broncs entered this year."

Gordon shrugged. "I'm not on the committee to contract stock for the circuit anymore. That job is now Daryl Buchanan's."

"Daryl Buchanan was one of the best bull riders on the circuit. He knows his bulls," Jesse said.

"Yes, he does. The board still reviews and approves contracts, but the board voted last year to have Buchanan have the final word."

"Hence your venture into working with broncs again?"

Gordon nodded. "Buchanan's fair. He wants healthy stock that perform well. If there's any doubt, he'll cancel the contract in favor of safety for all the animals and the riders."

"Then it's a good thing all the stock here are healthy," Jesse said before Carly could respond.

"Yes, I know. I saw your brother Sean with his new intern earlier today."

The announcer came over the intercom to announce the scores. Since the cowboy had been bucked off before the full eight second ride, the bull rider's score was zero. Carly held her breath as they gave the score for Tenacious.

"Score for Tenacious, forty-five," the announcer said.

Jesse whistled as Carly jumped up from her seat and clapped.

She turned to Gordon, who was still seated.

"Nice," Gordon said as he stood. "Congratulations again, Carly."

Carly watched Gordon walk away.

"It's going to be a problem if Daryl Buchanan finds out," she whispered, leaning into Jesse.

"Then he won't find out."

Jesse said himself that rodeo was a small world. Her ranch hands had been sworn to secrecy. But if word got out even in passing, it could get back to Daryl.

She glanced down the bleacher stairs until Gordon disappeared into a doorway that led to the area where the bulls were kept. "You want to bet money on that?"

# # #

Chapter Eight

This was her favorite time of the day. The sky was gradually getting darker. The world was getting quiet, although she could still hear the sounds of animals and people on the ranch. The air was getting cooler. And she'd just spent a glorious day doing what she loved with a man...

With an incredible man she couldn't stop thinking about. It almost made it easy to forget his reason for being here.

As she sat down on the top step of the porch, Carly fought to put thoughts of Jesse Knight out of her head as she recollected all the things that happened on a daily basis at night on the ranch. Doris was singing as she cleaned up the last remains of anything that needed straightening before she turned in. All the animals had been taken care of, and the ranch hands were now stopping for the day.

All the bulls had been put out to graze in the low pasture where Colin could keep a closer eye on them and prevent any accidental poisonings again. This time of the year, grazing was usually better on the higher pasture. But Carly had been very careful to make sure the pastures were continuously checked for any wild growth of toxic plants. This time of the year, weeds and wildflowers could grow as quickly as a flash fire. She and Jesse hadn't seen anything on their ride out the other day. But that didn't mean they hadn't missed something. At least on the lower pastures, she could be sure her bulls were safe.

She still clung to the hope that the poisonings of her bulls had been accidental. It happened. But that was just a fairytale. It would be too easy, especially in light of the two letters she'd received, to think otherwise. That was the only dark cloud on this beautiful night. Thank God there hadn't been another letter.

The familiar sound of laughing in the bunkhouse made her smile. The nightly card game had most likely commenced. It had been a nightly ritual for as long as Carly could remember. Her father had even sat in on a few games in the past and lost some money, making it talk amongst the hands for a week or so after. Except her father would quietly tell her that he'd lost on purpose just to boost morale.

It all seemed so normal and yet nothing around her was. She had a man living in her house who drove her crazy without doing a thing. All he had to do was look at her from across the room and she felt as though she'd come out of her skin. She was sure that everyone in the room could see it. Given her conversation with Doris this morning, she knew at least one person had.

She thought of all that had gone on this past year. Burying her father had been the worst. She wasn't sure she'd recovered from that. But really, how do you recover from the loss of a parent. Her father may not be walking the paths between the house and the barn or the bunkhouse, but he was all around her. Most days she wondered what he would think of the job she was doing at the Duggan Stock Company. Would he be proud?

"You look too serious for such a beautiful night."

Carly turned around and found Jesse standing a few yards away from her on the porch. "I didn't hear you come outside."

"I didn't. I was out in the pasture and then in the barn checking on feed containers. When I came back, I heard movement on the porch so I came around from the side to investigate."

She felt her insides hum. Some women wanted roses. Some wanted nights of dancing and sipping champagne with a handsome man. This cowboy checks on her stock as if they're his own and it melts her heart. *There was something truly wrong with her.*

"Thank you for that," she said.

He walked over to her and stopped at the rail leading down the steps. "It's nice tonight. Hardly any bugs."

She chuckled. "I noticed. It's cooler than it's been."

"I like it that way. When the night is cool, I sometimes like to sleep out under the stars. There's nothing like a Wyoming sky at night."

She glanced up at the sky. The moon was just a tiny sliver surrounded by millions of brilliant stars. In a few days there'd be a new moon. It brought back a bittersweet memory she hadn't thought of in a long time.

"When I was little, my mother and I would sit on the porch at night when I couldn't sleep. My father didn't like me getting out of bed after my bedtime. He was all about being regimented and running a tight ship. But my mom would smuggle me out of bed when she heard me playing in my bed instead of sleeping. Who knows, maybe she secretly wanted me to just be awake and keep her company. We'd come out here to the front porch like this so my dad wouldn't see us and just sit and watch the stars. My mom was a big science fiction buff. She loved all those sci-fi movies and books. She'd tell me how much she'd love to be an astronaut and fly to a different planet. After she died I wondered if when I looked up at the sky, she was up there on one of those stars smiling down at me. And then I felt as alone as she did."

"Your dad worked long hours like you?"

"More actually, if you can believe it. His job was all day, every day, and he loved it. My mom was lonely. As young as I was, I could tell. But they did love each other. And the times that I remember most with both of them was when we all went riding out on the property somewhere. Dad was still working, checking on the bulls or fencing, but we just had fun together. And then there were the times we went to a rodeo. I loved the excitement. I was never bored. Just like I was never bored here on the ranch. I mean, look at this? This was my playground. How can it get any better? But my mother was different."

"How so?"

"She grew up a rancher's daughter. She loved being on the ranch and I even think she even expected the loneliness. But I think she thought she'd have a big family to fill that void."

"I wonder why your parents didn't have a bigger family. You could certainly fill this house with enough kids to run a school."

Carly chuckled. "My mother had a hysterectomy a year after I was born. That's where the cancer started."

"Oh, that must have been rough on your mom."

"It was, but I never suspected anything until just before she died. The house was different when I was younger. My grandparents were still alive and of course, my mom. It feels strange with just me and Doris now. In fact, after seeing that big shopping Doris did before we left for the rodeo, I'm thinking she likes having you stay in the house. She tries to dote on me but..."

Carly sighed and looked up at the stars.

"She's like family, isn't she?"

"Yes. I know she could have left years ago. She was supposed to when I grew up. I didn't know that until a few years ago. My father hired her on as a nanny for me after my mother died. When my mom was still alive, and when Doris first came here, we had a housekeeper who came in every day to clean. But then I grew up and didn't need a nanny anymore and Doris just stayed. She's the only family I have left."

"What about Colin? He's been here on the ranch since you were little."

"True." She chuckled. "He's like an old uncle that sometimes let me do things my parents wouldn't let me do. It's been rough since my father died. He's known me ever since I had training wheels on my first bike. He was the one who took them off so I could take a test ride without them, much to my mother's dismay. She thought for sure I'd kill myself. I think that because I was an only child, they were a bit overprotective about some things and that spilled over to the way the ranch hands see me."

"They respect you as the head of the ranch. They take your lead."

"Do they? I wonder sometimes if the ranch runs because my father kept it like a well-oiled machine for so many years or if they're really looking at me as the head of the Duggan Stock Company. Sometimes I wonder if that's the reason this is happening now instead of on my father's watch. I doubt anyone would have tried this if he were still alive."

"You don't know that for sure. This rodeo circuit is tight."

"I know."

"Do you know that my family started the WRC over a hundred years ago?"

"Really? Is that true?"

Jesse sat down on the step next to her. "My great, great grandfather was one of the cowboys who started the circuit."

"I knew your father was on the board. But I didn't realize generations of Knights were a part of the WRC. So that means you have a vested interest in making sure there are no problems that would taint its name?"

"Something like that. I know a lot of people don't realize that, given my parent's ranch is nothing to look at compared to some of the stock companies that work with the rodeo. But the family is still involved and we've always had a bit of pride for how the WRC got started. Michael manages the small ranch my parents owned."

"Is your mom still there?"

"Yes. When Michael got married some years ago, he purchased a good spread next to my parent's property. It's pretty land up near Billings. Gordon Matthews bought a spread on the other side of my parent's ranch. That's how he knows my family so well. He's a neighbor."

"I didn't realize that either."

"If you had, would you have let me on your property that first day?"

She opened her mouth intending to say yes, but that wouldn't be honest. "I probably would have been more wary of you being here than I was."

The deep chuckle that rumbled in his chest sounded pleasing "I like that you're honest."

"So your family started the circuit, but then what?"

"What do you mean?"

"Your dad was part of the rodeo, just like you and your brother Michael. Was he a bull rider, too?"

"In the day, yes. He stopped when he injured himself. My uncle went PBR like Michael, and competed nationally. My dad fell in love and married my mom."

Her heart melted. "That's really sweet. But there are a lot of married people competing on the rodeo circuit."

"He competed early on. But then Michael was born, followed by me and then Sean. Three young toddlers under four was more than my mom could handle on her own so dad quit. He missed the rodeo but said he would have missed all the moments we had together as a family more."

"And you? What made you quit the rodeo?"

"I'm not a perfect man, Carly. I know none of us are but..."

"What?"

"I loved being a bull rider. I wouldn't trade those years. I made a lot of friends and I made some money. But I was looking at my brothers and seeing that there was something in their lives that I didn't have. And it hit me that I wasn't going to get it unless I made some changes in my life."

"And did you? Did the military give you that?"

He looked out onto the ranch and smiled. "For a while. Being a marine made me focus. It was a different kind of focus than riding bulls. But then I became an MP and that type of regiment was different. Crimes are committed everywhere, even in the military, sad as it is. I liked pulling things apart and getting to the core of an incident, bringing someone to justice if that be the case."

"So I'm definitely in good hands with you."

He glanced at her. Even though it was dark outside, she saw the contours of his face change and his lips stretch wide into a smile. "I'd like to think so."

He held her gaze for a long time. She focused on the little light that shown in the corner of his eye, making it glisten like the stars, and wondered where that light was coming from. It didn't matter. She liked looking at Jesse Knight. She liked being close to him. She didn't feel alone, which was ridiculous because she wasn't alone on the ranch. At any given time, the ranch was crawling with people.

But in the short time that they'd been together, Jesse had filled something inside her that had been missing for too long. And she realized as her heart started beating faster and her fingers itched to reach up and touch his face, that maybe she'd never had it at all.

"Why didn't you stay in the military? If you loved it so much, I mean," she asked.

"The void wasn't filled. I was still searching. For what I don't know."

She drew in a slow breath and then let it out slowly. "Do we ever know?"

"I hope so. I think some people do. I envied my brothers for knowing."

A thought occurred to her that shouldn't have made her feel sad, but did. "So coming here is just a stop on the road to finding something that fills that void."

Jesse reached up and touched her cheek. Carly melted into his touch and felt herself floating. "I may have found it."

She couldn't see his face but Carly felt the heat from his body. The cooler night air made it easier for her to feel him move closer. She wanted Jesse to kiss her. She'd thought about it many times since he'd dropped his boots on her ranch a week ago. How could she feel so much pull toward a man she'd only just met?

And then his lips met hers with a passion that exploded inside her and set her on fire. Carly wasn't a young girl at twenty-eight. Nor was she naïve about men. But she'd never felt so much so quickly for any man before.

Reaching up with her hand, she gripped his shoulder and fell against him, reveling in the warmth of his embrace and wanting him to be close. Closer. He made no move to part from their kiss and she was glad. She could spend the entire evening like this and still want more of him.

She felt the rise and fall of Jesse's chest with every caress of his hand against her back. Then his tongue teased her lips, wanting entrance, wanting more of her. And she was glad to give it.

A round of thunderous laughing jolted her back to reality. The men in the bunkhouse were far enough away that they couldn't see her kissing Jesse on the porch. But their presence was an intrusion of the intimacy between them all the same.

"Please don't tell me I shouldn't have done that," Jesse said.

She smiled up at him and touched his cheek, feeling the light stubble of hair on his chin. "Now why would I do that?"

He chuckled low. "I can't think of a single valid reason."

He kissed her again. This time slowly and with more passion. It wasn't the time for romance. But oh, it felt so right.

"You are one amazing woman, Carly Duggan," he said, holding her close and whispering against her ear.

"You think so?"

"I know so."

They spent the next hour holding each other on the porch, kissing and looking up at the stars. Carly spotted a shooting star and made a wish that time could stand still. She didn't want to live in danger, but she didn't want Jesse to leave either. And he would eventually. There'd be no reason for him to stay once they discovered who was responsible for poisoning her bulls and sending her death threats.

But for tonight, all of that was as distant as the stars above them. Tonight, she was happy to just be in Jesse's arms.

# # #

Chapter Nine

Two nights of sneaking alone time with Carly hadn't been enough for Jesse. Everything about the two of them was a complete surprise.

He loved holding her. He loved kissing her even more. And he wanted so much more, but that would have to wait. He couldn't allow his feelings for Carly to get in the way of doing what he needed to do to protect her. If he let his guard down too far, it would be easy for someone else to move in.

Stoney and Melanie had arrived to drive with the bulls up to Michael's ranch in Montana. The young bulls would only stay for a few hours. They'd let the bulls graze and get their fill of water before loading them up in the trailer and bringing them back. Before bulls could compete on the circuit, they needed to become comfortable with traveling in the trailer and being in a different environment. If they couldn't handle it, they couldn't compete.

"Stoney and Melanie are getting ready to take the bulls on a trailer ride up to Billings. Michael will meet us there. We'll do it again like we did for the rodeo," Jesse said as he walked into the kitchen and found Carly standing by the kitchen island, filling her bag with snacks and bottled water to take on the trip.

She grabbed the jar of hand cream from the counter and paused as she started to put it in her bag. Putting the hand cream back down on the counter, she reached inside the bag and pulled out an identical jar of hand cream.

"Huh. I must have already put one in my bag." She dropped the jar back inside the bag and grabbed the jar that was on the counter. After she opened it, she performed her usual ritual of slathering her hands and wrists.

"I swear you do that just to let me know where you are on this ranch," he said. "I smell that in the house and I come running."

"Are you implying I smell, Mr. Knight?" she said, taking a little more of the cream from the jar and smoothing it on her lower arm.

"It's a nice fragrance. I always know when you've been in the room because the scent lingers."

He'd come to love the smell of her. It was nothing heavy or filled with perfume. It was just there, a part of her, as if she was part of the fresh air after a rain.

"It's just eucalyptus and spearmint."

He watched her as she blended the cream into her skin, gently smoothing it over her fingers and palms and then the back of her hands, rubbing the excess up her arms.

"Does this entertain you?" she asked, watching his face.

Jesse felt the smile pull at his lips. A smile that betrayed the more sensual thoughts that were flowing through his mind. "More than you know."

She chuckled softly. "You men are all alike."

Her words sobered him. "You men? How many men have watched you put cream on your hands like this?"

Her eyebrows slid up her forehead just a bit. "Jealous?"

"Yes," he said quickly. "Does that bother you that I'd rather be the only man who's watched this little ritual of yours?"

"It intrigues me."

"Intrigues you. How?"

She crinkled her nose as she looked at him. "Don't you mean why?"

"I know why."

"Do you mind telling me..." Her face changed suddenly, and she glanced down at her hands.

"What's wrong?"

Carly said nothing for a few seconds. "Ah, nothing."

"I don't believe you. Tell me."

Jesse advanced toward Carly, suddenly forgetting his enjoyment over her bathing in hand cream. He was about to take her hands in his, but she pulled away and screwed the cap back on the jar. Then she set it on the center of the island. "It's nothing. I just..."

"What?"

"My hands feel like they're tingling. I've never had that feeling before" She picked up the jar of lotion and glanced at the back of it as if searching for ingredients. "There must be a lot of eucalyptus and spearmint in this jar."

He turned her around and placed his hands on her cheeks. After taking a brief moment to look down into her eyes, he kissed her moist lips. He loved kissing her. He loved the way she made a soft little noise in her throat when she was turned on and wanted more. He loved the way she melted into him, fitting against him like hand and glove.

But then she pulled away and took a deep gasp of air.

"What? Too much?"

"No. No, of course not."

He touched her arm but she wrenched it away, placing her hand over her chest.

Confused, he said, "This isn't quite the reaction I thought I'd get from a kiss."

"I'm sorry." Carly took a step back and touched her forehead.

"Don't be. I want to know what's wrong."

"I don't know. I...I don't feel good, Jesse." She placed her hand on her forehead again. His gaze followed her movement and he saw that beads of sweat bubbled up on her cheeks and forehead right before his eyes.

"Talk to me."

"I..." She took a deep breath and placed her hand on her chest. "I...don't feel very good. My chest."

Her skin turned ashen and her eyes rolled back in her head.

"Carly? Carly!"

Jesse had just enough time to slip his arm around her waist so Carly wouldn't collapse to the floor. Instead, he eased her down and placed his hand beneath her head.

"Doris?" he called out to the housekeeper. He knew she was somewhere downstairs. He'd heard her singing. "Doris, come quick!"

He heard nothing and wondered where the old woman had gone off to. Checking Carly's pulse, he was only mildly relieved to feel something. It was faint. But it was *something*.

Doris ran down the hall into the kitchen. Her face registered panic when she saw Carly sprawled out on the floor.

"Oh, no. My Carly. What has happened to my girl?"

"Call 911!" Jesse yelled. Doris stood frozen with her hands on her cheeks and her eyes wide as saucers. "Now, Doris. She's dying!"

Doris ran to the other side of the kitchen where the landline phone was connected. A 911 call from the landline would come up with the address, making it easier for paramedics to identify where to go without Doris having to relay the information.

"I need help," Doris cried into the phone. "My Carly has collapsed. We need an ambulance!"

Jesse kept his hand beneath Carly's head as he bent down and placed his ear over her heart. He heard it beating. But it wasn't the steady thump of a healthy heart. Still, the slight rise and fall of her chest, however labored it appeared to be, meant that Carly was still alive and breathing.

"Stay with me, baby. Don't leave me." He smoothed back her hair and wiped the beads of sweat from her face with the palm of his hand. "They'll be here soon. Help will be here soon. Don't worry," he whispered.

But Carly couldn't hear him. As he spoke, Jesse knew the words he uttered were to calm an indescribable fear that was paralyzing him. He wanted to believe help would be here soon to save Carly from whatever had happened. But seeing her normally sun kissed pink cheeks turn to gray, he knew life was slipping away from her rapidly, and he wasn't convinced help would make it in time to save her.

"Don't leave me," he whispered.

* * *

Two paramedics had set up an IV line right on the kitchen floor and then lifted Carly onto the stretcher. The older of the two turned to Jesse and asked, "What was she doing prior to falling ill."

Jesse thought back to those precious moments. He needed details. What had happened? "She put on some hand cream. She said her hands tingled and…"

"And what?"

"I kissed her."

The paramedic's face showed a flash of amusement, but instead of ribbing him, he nodded to the jar on the counter. "I doubt it was the kiss or you would have fallen ill too. Is that what she was putting on?"

Jesse nodded.

"Bring it with you. She might have had a reaction to one of the ingredients in the lotion and the ER doctor might want to have the cream analyzed."

The likelihood of Carly having a reaction like this to cream she'd been using for years was next to zero. Unless…

Jesse grabbed a paper towel and used it to make sure the jar was fully sealed. Then he searched for a paper bag to put the hand cream in.

He'd been in the house the whole time. Right here with her. Thinking back to Carly's surprise that she'd "already" had a jar of cream in her bag, it suddenly made sense. Someone had left it here on purpose. Someone knew she used this cream.

Doris walked next to Carly and cried as the paramedic pushed the stretcher to the open front door. As Jesse walked out the door behind them with the bag in his hand, he saw all the ranch hands lined up on the walkway staring at Carly.

Thad looked as if he were about to cry. "Is she going to be okay," he asked the paramedic.

The paramedic shrugged. "We'll have to see what the doctor says."

Jesse knew he didn't need to know what had caused Carly to collapse. He had the evidence right here in his hand. He was convinced of it. But looking at all the hands watching Carly get put in the ambulance, he realized he was no closer to figuring out who it was that had decided to wage war on this ranch.

But if it were the last thing he ever did, he'll be damned if he didn't find out. And when he did, God help whoever was responsible.

* * *

Jesse had driven in the truck with Melanie and Stoney on the way to the hospital. Doris was so upset, he let her drive in the ambulance with Carly. She was, by Carly's own admission, Carly's only family. Carly would have wanted it that way. He was sure of it. That didn't mean that every mile they drove to the hospital was easy. He hated not knowing what was going on inside that ambulance. He couldn't bear the thought of reaching the emergency room only to find out that Carly was dead.

They pulled up to the emergency room door behind the ambulance and he bolted out of the truck. He reached the back door of the ambulance just as the paramedics opened the door. When they pulled the stretcher out of the ambulance and lifted it, he saw that Carly's eyes were barely open and she had an oxygen mask on her face. She was still alive!

"I'm here, Carly," he called out to her as they quickly brought her inside. He followed Doris through the automatic doors, but they were stopped by a nurse.

"Please stay in the waiting room for now. The doctor will come out if he needs to talk to you."

Jesse handed the nurse the bag with cream in it. "I think this is what might have poisoned her."

"Poisoned?"

"Yes, she was using this right before she collapsed. Be careful with it."

The nurse took the bag. "I'll give it to the doctor."

* * *

After two agonizing hours of waiting, Dr. Stern finally came out into the waiting room. He appeared tired. But the slight smile on his face immediately put Jesse at ease.

"Mr. Knight?"

"That's me," Jesse said standing up to greet the doctor.

"I'm glad you brought in that jar of hand cream. The lab analyzed it. Things could have been so much worse if we hadn't known what had caused Ms. Duggan's heart to react the way it had."

"Her heart? She had a heart attack?" Doris asked with a whimper.

"No. We got her heart rate under control. But the substance in the cream is what caused her body to react the way it had. Her skin just absorbed it as fast as ingesting it."

"What caused it?" Melanie asked.

The doctor's voice as well as his face was filled with confusion. "Aconitum."

"Aconite?" Jesse asked.

Melanie said, "Monkshood. It's a pretty flowering plant that looks harmless but can be highly toxic to animals."

"And people," Dr. Stern said. "I have no idea how it got inside her hand cream, but it was highly toxic and it could have killed her. If you all hadn't reacted as quickly as you did, I'm afraid she'd be dead."

Doris cried out. "When can I see my girl?"

"You can go in right now. She's asking for you all. But I only want one person at a time in there and only for a few minutes. Her body has gone through an ordeal and she needs rest."

Doris wasted no time going into the emergency room. Jesse wanted to follow her. But he'd wait his turn.

"How would Carly have been exposed to aconite?" Stoney asked.

Dr. Stern frowned. "Believe it or not. Aconite is sometimes used in eastern medicine in very low doses. Some holistic treatments include aconite. But it's very dangerous if it's used without knowing exactly how much is being administered. Even low doses can be fatal. Wackos sell this stuff on the Internet and then people end up in the ER. If they're lucky they survive. Carly was lucky."

"Thank you, Doctor," Jesse said. He didn't bother correcting Dr. Stern's assumption that using cream with aconite was something Carly had done intentionally. He knew better. Whoever did this wasn't looking for a holistic cure to aging. They wanted Carly dead.

\# \# \#

Chapter Ten

It had been two long days that Carly had spent in the hospital. Two days she didn't want to revisit again in her life. When Carly thought about how close she'd come to death, it was enough to stop her heart as it nearly did when she'd collapsed in the kitchen.

Thank God Jesse had been there. The jar of cream from her bag that Melanie had analyzed after they'd learned the hospital found aconite in the cream turned out to have a higher concentration of the poison than the jar she'd used when she'd collapsed. It was just dumb luck that she'd chosen to use the jar on the counter instead of the jar in her bag.

A cold shiver raced through her as Jesse took her by the arm and helped her climb into bed. The doctor said it would be a few more days until she had her full strength back. She hoped it came back quickly. She'd already lost days of work at the hands of a lunatic.

"How do you feel?" Jesse asked, taking Carly's hand and pressing it against his cheek. His face had a light covering of stubble and it scratched her skin. But Carly didn't mind. She liked the feel of him. The strength of his touch. His warm embrace that made her feel small and safe in a way she thought she'd never feel again. And when she was with him, she wasn't alone. Even when he wasn't in the room.

She didn't want him to leave. He would be soon if they learned who it was who'd poisoned her and her bulls. That would be a sad day for sure.

He tipped her chin up with his fingers as she sat up in bed. "Why so sad? Are you really not feeling well?"

"I feel a whole lot better than I did the last time I was home," Carly said with a weak smile. "I feel a whole lot better when you're here. I felt so alone at that hospital without you."

A hundred emotions flashed across his face and she wondered if she'd said the wrong thing. Carly didn't have a lot of experience dating men. She'd always been so busy, and quite frankly, what man in his right mind wanted to face Zebb Duggan?

But she did know men, and Jesse was clearly fighting something.

"I thought..."

"What?" As her insides churned with anticipation, she noticed the tears filling his eyes.

"I really thought I was going to lose you."

She swallowed the emotion that choked her. "You very nearly did. Not that it was by choice."

"No. You had no hand in that."

She chuckled at the pun he didn't seem to get. "One would argue my hands were definitely part of it."

She knew the moment he understood when his lips stretched into that handsome smile she'd come to love. "Speaking of which."

She frowned as he got up from the bed and walked over to her vanity. He picked up a purple jar and brought it back to the bed. Then he sat down next to her.

"I found another jar of cream on your vanity so I had it analyzed. Same thing, just in a smaller concentration. That could be the reason you were feeling a little sick that day we drove to Bozeman."

"You could be right. It was a full jar. I mean, I know I've been a bit obsessive about my hand lotion, but even I don't buy three jars of hand cream at one time."

"It got me thinking."

"Yeah?"

"I think it's time you switched your hand cream." He handed her the jar and turned it so she could see.

Carly glanced at the jar. "Lavender."

"As much as I loved the spearmint scent, I think I'm traumatized for life. No more tingling. And no one gets to know about this cream. Deal?"

"Deal."

She opened the jar and took a deep whiff of the lavender scent.

"Is it girly enough for you?" he asked with a half grin.

"It is for me if it is for you. Thank you." She leaned forward and wrapped her arm around his shoulder. "I love having you here. I'm going to hate it when you have to leave."

"Ssh. We don't have to think about that tonight. Just get some rest. Do you want me to have Doris bring you some tea?"

"No." Carly glanced at the clock. It was just past nine-thirty. Doris was always in bed early. It had been an emotional few days for her as it had been for Carly. "She needs to rest too."

"I'll bring you a cup of tea after I check the grounds."

"Okay," she said, sinking back against the cool pillow. Her body melted against it as if in resignation. As Jesse closed her bedroom door and shut the light off, she closed her eyes and wondered if she'd even be awake when he returned.

* * *

The drive back from the hospital had taken its toll on Carly, Jesse thought as he walked through the quiet house. As Carly mentioned, Doris had already gone to bed. Jesse walked passed her closed bedroom door and saw no light peeking out from the threshold. There was also no sound from the TV.

He walked downstairs and through the main hallway towards the mudroom and checked the door to make sure it was locked. No one liked the new locked house policy. But that was too bad. No one was getting in this house without Jesse knowing about it.

Once he knew everything was secure, Jesse decided to head out to the barn. Too much time had gone by and he was afraid the trail had grown cold. They may never find out who poisoned Carly and the bulls. For all anyone knew, that person could be long gone by now.

Or they could still be lurking about on the ranch. A lot of ranches in Wyoming and Montana had a lot of acreage with plenty of places for someone to hide if they didn't want to be found. It was impossible for him to comb the entire ranch. But at the very least, he could make sure the perimeter was secure.

He locked the house and pocketed the key. Then he walked the length of the porch to the steps leading to the path that would lead him to the barn. Colin had been on watch in the barn all day to keep a close eye on Widow Maker, Tenacious and Cotton-Eye, which were being housed in an open area of the barn that led to the paddock where they were keeping the rest of the futurity bulls. Normally the herd would be left to graze overnight in the pastures. But it was too dangerous. They needed to have them close by.

Michael would be here tomorrow morning with Stoney and they'd move the prized bulls over to Black Rock to make sure no one could target them again. But that was only a quick fix. The rest of the bulls were still at risk with someone among their ranks.

The light in the barn was off and immediately made Jesse's stomach churn. In all the time he'd been at the ranch, the barn lights had never completely been turned off. One of the hands had always been in there and even if they weren't, the main overhead light was kept on overnight and still visible from outside.

Jesse pulled his cell phone out of his pocket. The front screen illuminated when he pressed the side button. On the home screen, he chose the flashlight app and waited for the beam to turn on before reaching for barn door. Once inside, he shined the light down the center aisle. The familiar scent of hay, oats and manure assaulted his nose. As he moved closer to the wall to feel for the light switch, the sound of animals moving inside their confined area grew louder. It would make it harder to hear movement from anyone lurking about.

Jesse flicked the light switch but nothing turned on. He slowly walked down the center aisle and stopped at the gated stalls that housed Cotton-Eye, Widow Maker, and Tenacious. All three bulls looked as they did earlier when he'd checked on them.

Where was Colin? He was supposed to be keeping an eye on...

Jesse stopped moving and listened. Amid the sounds of the animals moving, he heard a groan. He quickly shined the light in the direction he heard the noise. Each of the stalls he'd shined the light into were empty until he got to the second to last stall.

"Damn!"

Jesse grabbed the gate to the stall and swung it open, shining the light onto the ground where Colin was sprawled out on the floor.

"Colin?"

He shined the beam of light on Colin's head and saw the blood streaming down the side.

"I'm...I'm okay."

"Can you stand?"

"A bump on the head isn't gonna keep me down." Colin lifted his torso up off the ground and rested his weight on his elbow. Then he slumped back.

"Stay down," Jesse said. "You're liable to fall and hurt yourself worse than you already are."

"He...came out of nowhere."

Jesse turned as if someone was behind him. Someone that Colin could see but he couldn't?

"Who? Who did this?" Jesse said, feeling the heat rise up his neck and singe his skin beneath his collar.

Colin shook his head slightly and then put his hand over his forehead as if that would stop the spinning. "Didn't see him. The lights when out. I yelled to whoever was there to put them back on. But I never saw him. I walked...down the center aisle toward the tack room and then..." Colin chuckled. "Then the lights *really* went out."

"How did you get in the stall down here?"

Colin looked around. "Is that where I am? Beats me."

"Someone dragged you. Stay here," he said, handing Colin his cell phone. "Call 911. Tell them to send an ambulance."

"I don't need no ambulance."

"Let me be the judge of that. Tell them this time we need the police, too. I'm going to look around. Stay put and wait for them."

"No worries. Not sure I could move if I tried."

Jesse gripped Colin's upper arm. He wasn't sure if it was to give him reassurance or out of his own nerves. There was a killer out here on the ranch. He'd succeeded in killing an innocent bull and had tried mightily, and nearly succeeded, in killing a woman Jesse cared deeply about. And now he was back at the ranch to do God only knew what.

The bulls that had been in the open stall had moved through the open doorway into the paddock where the other bulls were grazing on hay. The sound of the animals being moved about drew Jesse's attention to the open paddock. Because the barn was dark, Jesse ran his hand along the rail of each stall and counted his way down the aisle until he reached the closed barn door. Pushing the door open was no better. There was no moon in the sky, making it harder to see in front of him.

Jesse waited a second for his eyes to adjust to being outside. He listened, but only heard the sound of hooves clopping on the dry dirt in the paddock and the occasional grunt from the bulls. Without the cell phone flashlight, it would make moving in the dark tricky. Movement among the herd played tricks with his eyes as he scanned the area. He gripped the wooden rail of the paddock and focused on the sounds he heard until he could distinguish the sound of hooves on the ground and those of a man.

The other ranch hands were playing cards in the bunkhouse. Jesse could hear Thad laugh. With Colin out in the barn, there probably weren't enough players for cards. Jesse listened again and heard the television blaring. And then something else. The sound of boots on the gravel path pulled his attention toward the house. *Quick steps.*

Jesse glanced in the direction of the bunkhouse. He hadn't heard a door shut. The men knew they were not allowed to go to the house at this time of the night, so that could only mean one thing.

Turning back to the house, Jesse ran as quickly as he could up the path, thankful that he'd left the porch light on when he'd left. Just as he reached in the pocket of his jeans for the key, he heard a window on the side of the house shatter, stopping him cold. He fumbled for just a few seconds in his haste to get the key in the lock. When he finally did, he wasted no time pushing through the door and racing through the house to the hallway leading to the mudroom, being careful to glance around as he went and turn on lights. He wanted whoever was here to know he was coming.

The door to the mudroom was closed. Jesse thought back to when he'd checked it early. Yes, he'd left it open. There was no reason for Doris to come into the mudroom at this time of the night. Carly had hardly any energy as it was, so Jesse knew it hadn't been her to come downstairs and close it.

His pulse pounded in his ear, deafening him in the silence around him as he eased the mudroom door open. He tried the light switch. But just like the barn, the lights wouldn't turn on. From the light in the hallway, Jesse saw the source of the shattered glass. Someone had broken the bottom window pane on the door to get into the house. Glass was all over the floor in front of the door, which was still slightly ajar.

He listened as he moved down the hall toward the staircase that led to the second floor sleeping quarters. But a noise coming from a room downstairs kept him from taking the first step upstairs.

Torn between checking on Carly and investigating the noise downstairs, he decided whoever broke in was probably still on the first floor. He passed the gun rack hanging on the wall and eased a rifle off quietly. Carly had told him once before that Zebb kept the house unlocked because everyone knew he kept his rifles loaded. They wouldn't dare cross him. Jesse didn't take the time to check as he crept down the hall past the living room and to Carly's office.

The door was closed. But a slice of light at the threshold told Jesse that someone was inside.

His heart hammered in his chest as he pushed through the office door.

"Don't come any closer."

It took a few seconds for Jesse to process who he was looking at. Rod Nolan was dressed all in black wearing a hooded sweatshirt and pants, not in the normal blue jeans and shirt he normally wore while working on the ranch.

"You don't have any part in this, Knight. Just let me get what I came for and then I'll leave."

"Do I have to ask what you're doing here? Or are you going to give it up yourself?" Jesse said, keeping the barrel of the gun pointed at Rod. "Because I have no problem with beating it out of you."

Rod was crouched down on the floor next to the liquor cabinet. "This is none of your business."

"Convince me. Because right now I'm not seeing it that way."

Rod stood up. In his hand he had a drill. "I don't need to convince you of anything. You're an outsider to this ranch. You show up here and act like you own the place. You know nothing of what's gone on here or what was promised before you arrived."

Jesse had no idea what Rod was talking about, but he had a good feeling it was at the root of poisonings and the death threats.

"Why don't you share that with me so I don't call the authorities."

Standing up straight and giving Jesse a cocky grin, he said, "Call the authorities? For what? You just found a ranch hand that's been working on this ranch for ten years in the owner's office doing chores."

"Chores? At this time of the night?"

"This ranch runs twenty-four/seven. Carly has us hands do chores all over this ranch. Even in the house. Who do you think they'll believe? The man who's worked his fingers to the bone for years or the man who just showed up on the scene out of thin air. You have no business here, Knight. Now get out and let me get on with this."

Jesse inched forward. "Carly has made it my business. That trumps whatever fabricated story you can make up."

His movement didn't sway Rod to retreat. In fact, Jesse could see Rod's face grow redder and his eyes wider.

"You just back up and shut the door, Knight. I'm going to get what I came here for and then I'm leaving. Anything you do to stop me will only make things end badly."

"How much worse can things get? You were the one who poisoned, Carly. You've known her since she was a teenager and you tried to kill her! If you think I'm going to let you just walk away from this, you'd better think again."

"I didn't know that cream was going to hurt Carly like that. It was only supposed to make her a little sick."

"Like Lighting Strikes? Was that poor bull only supposed to get sick, too?"

A flash of regret crossed Rod's face. But then his lips thinned and his expression became tight. "That wasn't supposed to happen. I didn't know how much to give him. It wasn't supposed to kill him."

"Well, it did," Jesse said, feeling the anger surge inside of him until he couldn't stand it. "And it nearly killed Carly! Why did you do this?"

He lifted the drill in his hand as if he was ready to use it as a weapon. "It's her own damned father's fault. He set this in motion long before you arrived."

# # #

Chapter Eleven

Jesse stared at Rod's face and saw the evil in his eye. "What are you talking about?"

"He's the one who promised us a share of the profits off Tenacious's winnings. Ten percent of the profits from that bull are supposed to be split with the ranch hands. But then he changed his damned will and left us nothing. That bull is making money. He's going to get a damned endorsement that could be worth…millions. We take care of the animal. We haul it back and forth to every rodeo on the circuit and the ranch makes all the money. We get nothing. He gets all the money and doesn't even keep his word."

It made no sense to Jesse. But criminal behavior was never rational.

Rod lifted his chin in defiance. "You think this is all me? Hell, I was hired to do this. If I wasn't going to get the money I was owed from this ranch, then I got me some money somewhere else."

"What are you talking about?"

"I didn't think it up on my own. If you think stopping me is going to stop trouble from coming to the WRC, then you're crazy. This is just the beginning."

But before Jesse could ask how, Rod leaned back against the liquor cabinet as if he lost his step. Jesse took a step forward, dropping the barrel of the rifle a few inches as he moved. In one quick movement, Rod reached behind him and threw something at Jesse. Jesse reacted, but he wasn't quick enough. He felt a sharp pain against the side of his head and the force of something pushing him over until he fell to his knees. Glass shattered around him and then he felt liquid seep into the fabric of his jeans where his knee touched the floor. The pungent scent of bourbon rose up to his face and made his stomach roll as the pain in his head throbbed.

Struggling to his feet, Jesse blinked once, twice and then made his way in the direction that Rod had just gone. He heard the front door swing open and smash against the wall as Rod bolted from the house. When Jesse reached the door, he saw Doris appear halfway down the steps.

She clutched her robe to her chest. "What in heaven's name is going on? Was that Rod I just saw?"

"Call the police and then go upstairs and stay with Carly!" he called up to her.

She gasped when she saw the blood streaming down the side of his face. He could feel it. He smelled the strong sent of blood invading his nostrils. By the look on Doris's face, Jesse figured it probably looked worse than it felt.

"Jesse! What happened to your face?"

"Just stay with Carly. Stay hidden!"

He sprinted out the door and jumped off the porch without taking any of the steps and ran down the path toward the barn. If Rod was desperate enough to poison bulls and to nearly kill Carly, then he was crazy enough to do anything. He saw a figure come running out of the barn and then stop. Jesse stopped running and pointed the rifle.

Colin turned to him and lifted his hands. His face registered pure shock as he looked down the barrel of the rifle. "Have you gone mad? It's me. I heard yelling in the house."

"Where's Rod. He was behind the poisonings."

"No! It can't be."

"He admitted it. Did you see him at all?"

"I heard someone head to the back where the hands keep their trucks parked."

"He's fleeing."

They both ran behind the barn to the bunkhouse. Red taillights blazed into the night. He heard the sound of the truck's engine firing to life and then the taillights change from red to white, indicating the truck was in reverse.

"That's his truck," Colin said. "That bastard. I'll—"

Jesse lifted the rifle and peered into the telescope.

"Good God, man. You're not going to shoot him, are you?" Colin said just as Jesse pulled the trigger and fired.

He knew the instant his bullet hit the back tire and deflated it. The truck pitched to one side. But Rod was undeterred. He continued to drive with a blown out tire. Jesse aimed the gun again as the truck shifted gears and then fired again, disabling another tire.

"Damn!" he heard Rod yell from inside the cab of the truck. The door flew open and Rod bolted into the pasture where the bulls were frantically moving around. Jesse handed the rifle to Colin.

"If you see him come out, shoot his knees."

Jesse ran in the direction he'd just seen Rod go. Normally bulls were fairly docile when they were in familiar surroundings. But the sound of the rifle discharging had scared them enough to make them run. In the dark it was hard to make out the images moving around him in the pasture.

He relied on his hearing, trying hard to distinguish the sound of hooves with the sound of a man's boots.

"Give it up, Rod. The game is over!" he called out.

Cotton-Eye was close by. Even in the darkness, Jesse could make out the white spot over his eye that was his signature. Jesse stayed close to Cotton-Eye and listened to the sounds above the groans of the bulls that had scattered.

"I just want what's mine, Knight. I don't want to cause any trouble."

"You've already done enough of that!" Jesse moved slowly through the pasture until he saw a cluster of bulls. He headed in that direction and was relieved when some of the bulls separated enough so he could see Rod using them as a shield.

Rod spotted him and then ran back toward the barn. Jesse took off after him, breathing hard and feeling every bit of rage over what this monster had done to the animals and the woman he cared deeply about. His head throbbed, but he didn't care. He kept his eyes fixed on the dark form moving quickly and ran toward it.

As if fate were stepping in, one of the bulls ran in front of Rod and plowed into him. Rod flew over the bull and then landed on the ground with a thud. When Jesse reached Rod, he found him writhing in pain from being run down by the bull.

Breathing hard, he peered down at Rod and said, "It's called payback, buddy. If that bull hadn't done it, I would have. And I would have enjoyed every minute of it after what you've done."

* * *

Carly wrapped the robe tighter around her waist. Standing on the porch, she peered over at the police cruiser flashing red and blue lights down her driveway and into the dark night. She watched as the paramedics put Rod into the back of the ambulance and shut the door.

"I can't believe it," Doris said, holding her hand against her cheek. "He seemed like such a nice boy. I can't believe he would do something like that."

As the ambulance pulled away, Carly replayed what Jesse had told her about finding Rod in the office and it only made her more confused. Her father never spoke to her about giving away shares of Tenacious. If he had…

Colin was standing with Jesse as they gave their statements of the night's events to a police officer.

"Carly?" Doris said as Carly took each step down off the porch and walked over to the men.

"Ma'am," the police officer said as she approached. "How are you feeling?"

"Fine. Thank you for coming out tonight."

"Are you up for questions?"

She turned to Colin. "Yes. But I have a few of my own first. Colin, is it true? Did my father promise the ranch hands a share in the earnings from Tenacious?"

Colin turned his attention to the ground, clearly uncomfortable with her question.

"None of that needs to be talked about tonight, Carly. The will gave—"

"Look at me, please." She waited until Colin looked her in the eye. "Did my father make that promise?"

"He mentioned it one night over a game of cards. He said that Tenacious was performing so well, he wanted to give the men a ten percent share they could split for all their hard work.

It was over a game of cards, Carly. I didn't think Zebb really meant it, especially in light of the will. But some of the men were sore about it."

She shook her head. "You know my father never said anything unless he meant it, Colin. If he wanted to give you and the other hands a share in Tenacious, then the paperwork is somewhere. We just have to find it. I'm sure that's what Rod was looking for in the office."

"Something like shares in the profits of a bull wouldn't be in a will unless Zebb Duggan knew he was dying," the police officer said. "Was he sick for a long time?"

"My father had a heart attack," Carly said. "He poured a cup of coffee in the kitchen one morning, turned to say something to me and Doris and he simply dropped. He had no idea he was going to die. Until that moment I would have sworn he was healthy as an ox."

"It's true," Colin said. "Zebb was a strong man."

She sighed. "And he was true to his word. Colin, why didn't you say something to me?"

"It wasn't my place."

"All this time I've felt this...tension with the ranch hands. Was this what it was all about?"

"There's been some questions among the men. But I told them to forget about it."

"No. That's not right. I trust your word, Colin. If my father told you he was going to give a share of profits from Tenacious to the ranch hands, then I'm going to honor that, even if I can't find any paper trail. It's only right."

Colin smiled. "You are truly your father's daughter, Carly."

Tears welled in her eyes. "Thank you for saying that."

The officer slapped his notepad closed. "Apparently Rod Nolan wasn't up for forgetting. He kept spouting off about getting money that he was promised." He turned to Colin. "I'd like to go talk to some of the other hands to see if he mentioned anything to them."

"I'll bring you to the bunkhouse," Colin said.

When they were alone, Jessie's expression grew more serious. She focused on the bandage the paramedic had put on his temple.

"Does your head hurt?"

"A little. But that's the least of my worries."

"What do you mean? You found out who was responsible for the poisonings. Rod admitted to the police he sent the letters. We don't have to worry about that anymore."

"He told me someone hired him."

"What do you mean? Who?" Carly asked.

"I don't know. He just laughed and said that I might stop him but he was only a small part of something bigger. He was only the tip of the iceberg. It wasn't going to end with him."

She frowned. "What did he mean by that?"

Jesse shook his head. "I have no idea. But I'm not leaving you until I know for sure you're out of danger."

Her heart lifted in her chest. "You don't want to leave?"

He pulled her into his arms and held her close. She felt his warmth, and swore she could feel his heart beating. "What do you think? I can't leave you."

She wrapped her arms around his waist and rested her cheek on his shoulder. "People leave all the time, Jesse. Whether they want to or not."

"I know. But I'm telling you right now that I don't want to. I've never felt like this before, Carly. I've never been so scared as I was tonight."

"Of course you were. You had a crazy man try to kill you tonight."

"It wasn't about me. I was afraid for you. He got into the house, Carly. He could have easily gone upstairs and finished what he'd started. If I'd found you... I couldn't bear it."

"He didn't go upstairs. He went to the office. I have no idea what he was looking for."

"Rod was trying to get into the safe. He had a drill."

She chuckled, although she felt no humor. "He wouldn't have gotten far with a drill. That safe is as secure as Fort Knox. My father had it specially made."

"He was probably trying to find paperwork that would prove he owned a share of Tenacious."

"Or maybe more money."

She felt the rise and fall of Jesse's chest as he held her tighter. "That's what scares me the most. He said someone paid him to do this. He said if he couldn't get the money owed to him from Tenacious, then he was prepared to take it any way he could."

She pulled away and looked at his face. "Who would hire him to do this? Why would anyone outside this ranch even care about a deal my father made with the ranch hands?"

"I don't know. He just laughed and said this was just the beginning."

"Who do you think he's talking about?"

"It could be anyone." He brushed her cheek with his knuckles and then bent his head and kissed her lips. "I want you in my life. You fill a part of me that I didn't know needed filling."

"I feel the same way."

"Yeah? I'm falling in love with you, Carly. Even if all the danger ended tonight and I knew you'd be fine, I'd still want to be here. I don't know what the future holds. I just know that I want you to be in it. I love having you like this in my arms. I love looking into your eyes and seeing something beautiful. You are so beautiful. I'm...I'm not falling in love with you. I am in love with you, Carly Duggan."

Her heart swelled. "I feel the same way. You make me feel special, Jesse. I don't want you to leave either. I don't know what the future holds, but whatever lies ahead, I want you to be with me."

He held her tight and for the first time since her father died, she felt as if she weren't alone. What they felt for each other was still so new, but it had a promise for a beautiful future that Carly never thought was possible. Together they could figure out the rest. All Carly cared about as Jesse held her is that she finally felt at home again, in his arms.

The End

Don't miss out!

Visit the website below and you can sign up to receive emails whenever Lisa Mondello publishes a new book. There's no charge and no obligation.

https://books2read.com/r/B-A-CEU-XQNH

BOOKS 2 READ

Connecting independent readers to independent writers.